P9-ECV-984

Turning The Corner

Turning
The Corner

by Ruth Schiffman

 THE DIAL PRESS · NEW YORK

Published by
The Dial Press
1 Dag Hammarskjold Plaza
New York, New York 10017

LIBRARY OF CONGRESS CATALOGING IN PUBLICATION DATA
Schiffman, Ruth.
Turning the corner.
SUMMARY: A graduating high school senior struggles
to make a future for herself during the Great Depression.
[1. Jews in the United States—Fiction.
2. Depressions—1929—Fiction]   I. Title.
PZ7.S34615Tu   [Fic]   80–25887
ISBN 0–8037–9153–4

Chapter 1

It was the first Thursday of September. Mama, Papa, and I sat at breakfast, dipping Mama's cinnamon buns in sweet milky coffee, while I worried about the first weekend of my senior year in high school.

This morning, as usual, Mama had a suggestion for improving my social life. "Why don't you hang out your blue dress on the line? So it will be fresh for Saturday night. The dance."

"Oh, Ma, I hate those dances. The basement of the *shul* is always damp. And the boys are all too short."

"Maybe this time it will be better."

"And maybe a fairy godmother will change my old dress into a new one." Other girls, I thought, had smart new clothes, while I was still wearing the dress that had been bought more than three years before for Samuel's Bar Mitzvah.

"You'll look nice no matter what you wear."

"Leave her be, Sophie. If she doesn't like the dance, why should she go?"

I was grateful that Papa had stopped Mama. I was tired of reminding her that there were no more than a dozen Jewish boys in Forgetown, and it seemed as if there were three girls for each of them.

Ever since I was old enough to know about weekends, I had hated them. Not one ever kept its Friday promise. I, Rebecca Levine, would soon be seventeen and I had never had a date. No boy had held my hand walking down Broadway or bought me a soda at the Sweet Shop. No one but my kid brother, Samuel, had ever taken me to the movies. Even though Forgetown, Pennsylvania, like the whole rest of the country, was in the middle of a Depression, other girls had dates: pretty girls with pale skin and freckles and fine blond hair that curled up at the ends. Even girls with frizzy hair had dates. I wondered if I had some terrible odor that survived all my scrubbing and brushing.

As I thought of the year ahead I had trouble swallowing even the coffee-softened pastry, for yawning at the end of another year of dateless weekends was my Senior Prom. Unless my life took a sudden turning, there would be no one I could ask to take me to the dance. In June, 1936, the whole senior class would be together and would learn that no one wanted to spend an evening with me.

Upstairs we could hear Samuel's dresser drawers being

opened and closed as he hastily searched for clean clothes. We did not move when the screen door opened and we heard footsteps going into our living room, for this was a regular part of our mornings. Heshie Greenspan, Samuel's best friend, had arrived to go with him to school.

I swallowed the last drops of coffee and gathered my books as Samuel, who had come downstairs in a series of clumps, was spreading Mama's strawberry jam on toast to eat on his way to school. At her urging, he was gulping a glass of milk as I waved to Heshie on my way out the door. Halfway down the block, a loud slam signaled that the boys had left the house. Calling back and forth to each other, they ran past me down the hill.

I reached Broadway, my morning meeting place with my best friend, Janet Somerset, just as she arrived at the intersection. Linking arms, we walked the rest of the way to school; both of us taller than most of the other senior girls, Janet with a full pink-cheeked face and straight honey-colored hair and I, olive-skinned with brown eyes and dark brown too-curly hair that would never lie flat.

After school I had an important errand. I hurried to the library where, I often thought, I must be the best customer, to pick up my weekend supply of books.

Mrs. Mott, the head librarian, smiled as she leaned across the counter. "I don't think you've read this, Rebecca," she said, handing me a large blue book.

ANTHONY ADVERSE was stamped in red on the buff-colored binding. I hefted the book, pleased with its weight, for it would fill more hours than a slim, delicate volume.

At Saturday breakfast, so Mama would not mistakenly assume I was going to the dance, I told her that I was going to the movies with Samuel and Heshie. We all knew how much Samuel loved the movies. Mama deplored the time and money spent on such foolishness. "A book," she would say, scolding Samuel. "Why don't you read a book?"

"Books are dull. Movies are exciting."

"Hundreds of years men are reading books, learning everything from books. But to you, 'Books are dull.' "

"You think, because people have learned from books before, that they always will. Did you ever think, someday people will learn from the radio? Or even the movies?"

" 'Someday.' Don't give me 'someday.' It's 'now' now. And anybody who wants to be somebody has to read books and get good marks in school."

Sitting between Samuel and Heshie at the Plaza Theatre, I thought about Mama's words. Heshie did not have to worry about doing well in school. His father owned the largest liquor store in town. Perhaps it was hard times that made people think they had to have a bottle in the house in case of real trouble. But whatever the reason, Myron Greenspan's store was always busy. Heshie's family would not need him to help support them, as we needed Samuel.

But Samuel was only a sophomore who had shown scant liking for school or books. There was little chance that he would be able to find a job that would support him and allow him to help our parents.

I sucked on a spearmint leaf—at five for a penny, the

best value in the Sweet Shop—trying to make it last, as I succumbed to the flickering images on the screen. The shadowy figures in full evening dress, traveling in sleek automobiles were not as real to me as those I visualized when I read a book, but watching them helped me to forget drab Forgetown. When the movie ended, the three of us climbed back up the hill, talking of Jean Harlow and John Barrymore.

On Monday morning, as I walked to meet Janet, I tried to imagine what life would be like without school. School shaped my days. There my life was full of material for fashioning daydreams. First period each morning I was a beautiful countess, entertaining—in the battlemented castle on the end pages of my textbook—the fearless knights who dueled for my hand. I studied charts of municipal, state, and federal governments in civics class and pictured the headlines when I was named the first woman Justice of the Supreme Court. As I dissected my frog I saw my name on the cover of a treatise about vertebrate structures.

Bookkeeping class on the other hand was no subject for dreams. It was a forced march to form the digits with clarity and to marshal the figures in lockstep. Hand-to-hand combat with the rows was necessary to balance each to the last penny. Nevertheless, since the previous autumn, it had seemed that bookkeeping might be my destiny.

Not knowing another way to find a job, I had gone to Papa's shop after school. He sat at his machine, rhythmically pumping the foot treadle, as his long-fingered hand fed the seams of a brown wool skirt under the needle.

"Ah, Rebecca, you want maybe a cup of coffee? In the back, on the sill, there's milk." The scent of the coffee that simmered all day on the back of the coal stove filled the small store. I busied myself fixing coffee in Papa's big white cup with lots of milk and sugar, so that it was really sweet, coffee-flavored milk.

My embarrassment hidden by the activity with the spoon and cup, I was able to speak about what had brought me there. "Papa, is there someone you can ask about a job for me?"

"Are you sure, Rebecca, it wouldn't make you sick? Working while you go to school?" Papa had stopped pumping, and now the hum of the machine, like the smell of coffee, an essential characteristic of the shop, was stilled.

"I'm strong as a horse, like you. And besides," I lied, "I get bored after school."

"I never thought it would be that my children would have to work while they were still in school . . . but who could know such times? Uncle Ellenbogen told me—in his little store, you remember, just greeting cards and a soda fountain—sometimes two, three times a week, grown men come in to ask does he have a job. Sweeping, packing, anything. He says he gives them a roll and butter. Sometimes, even, they put it away to take home. What else can he do? He doesn't have work for more than one person."

"Papa, I know the Depression hurts everyone, not just us. And it's all right if I work. Honest."

Papa got up from his machine to hug me. "I'll ask

Mrs. Wallington," he said. "She comes today for a fitting."

Of all Papa's customers Mrs. Wallington was the best. A big double-breasted woman, he had told us, describing her after her first visit to his shop. " 'Mr. Levine, I am hard to fit,' " he had reported her saying to him. "So I told her I could make for her a suit so she would look important, not fat."

The suit, navy blue wool crepe with eggshell-silk collar and cuffs, had accomplished what Papa had promised. Every spring and fall after that he had duplicated his feat. We could live for more than a month on what Mrs. Wallington paid Papa for one suit.

That night, a woman's voice on the telephone asked for Mr. Levine. I handed the phone to Papa. "Yes. Thank you. Yes. I understand. Thanks anyway," we heard. "This week the Works cut back to three and a half days," Papa told us. "Mrs. Wallington was not a good one to ask."

On Papa's second try he was luckier. Harry Goldstein of the Smart Set said he could use me. He would pay four dollars a week for two hours a day after school and all day Saturday. After school and on Saturday mornings I would be a bookkeeper. As soon as I learned the stock, on Saturday afternoons I would help to sell blouses and skirts, stockings and brassieres.

Throughout the previous summer I had worried what would happen to the hundred and seven of us who would graduate in June. It was not only Forgetown—no place in the country seemed to need last year's graduates or the graduates of previous years. I remembered the line of unemployed men that I had seen the previous spring when we had gone to a Seder at Tanta Ellenbogen's in Brooklyn. On its way to the soup kitchen on the avenue, the line had wound twice around the block. The men slowly shuffled by, not lifting their heads, looking to me as though they could not remember what it was like to eat a meal at a table with a family.

Just last week at the freight yard the police had arrested a fifty-one-year-old man for vagrancy. An accountant, he had lost a job he had held in Utica for twenty-two years. Since 1931 he had been unable to find another and had lived in empty freight cars. Every day seemed to bring another story of a friend or relative in Pittsburgh, or Detroit, or Chicago who, no matter where he tried, could not find work.

Papa blamed Mr. Roosevelt for not doing more. A man should not be treated like a thief or an outcast, Papa said, because the company he worked for failed. He should not be punished for economic conditions in the country—in the world, for that matter—that were not of his doing. No government had the right to stand by and let its people starve.

Not everyone agreed with Papa. Mr. Somerset, Janet's father, had different ideas. Ever since I had known Janet, when we were both in the second grade, her father had been plant manager of the Forgetown Iron Works. The Somersets lived on the other side of Broadway, farther up the hill from Easton Street, where the houses always seemed newly painted. The Somersets' furniture was newer and shinier than ours, except for some of the things that I had been told were antiques from Georgia, where Mr. Somerset's family lived. Whenever I was a guest there, Mr. Somerset shook my hand and asked after my mother's health, although he had never met her. If I was invited for dinner, we ate in the dining room as though the Somersets did so every night, not just Fridays or holidays as we did at home.

During the last days of August I was at the Somersets' dinner table when Mr. Somerset learned that their next door neighbor's son had joined the Civilian Conservation Corps.

"Con-ser-*va*-tion," he had said over a low bowl of flowers, his syllables carefully separated, with iron underlining his drawl. "Roosevelt must think we are all fools."

"But the CCC uses boys without jobs to save the trees in our national parks," I said.

"My dear, you have fallen right into his trap. That is pre-*cise*-ly what he wants you to think. But it is an army nevertheless. He is getting all the young men in camps so he can use them to take businesses from their owners and run them himself. Thank the Lord, we only have to wait one year more until we can vote him and his pernicious foreign ideas out of Washington."

"But don't we need the WPA and the PWA for people who want jobs but can't find them?"

"Lies, lies. Any man who really wants to work, can. Those post offices, and courthouses, and dams; all those 'public works' are just another way of taking money from hardworking people and giving it to loafers who lean on shovels."

I believed, as Papa did, that sometimes President Roosevelt favored big businesses and farm owners in-

stead of small ones and sharecroppers. Many in Forgetown, however, agreed with Mr. Somerset that the President's programs were dangerously close to Socialism;
they hated and feared them for suggesting changes from
the ways of their parents and grandparents. But I thought
that a job, even one in a public works program, as long
as it let a man look up when he walked instead of down
at his feet, was still a good thing to have.

By Sunday afternoon there was so much of autumn and
expectation in the air that *Anthony Adverse* could not
keep me home. The day was bright and clear; perfect
weather, I thought, for other girls walking with boys
from school. I left the house, ran down the hill, and followed Easton Street along the river to the one place
where I could sit without trespassing. In the Jewish cemetery was the only land the Levines had ever owned: the
grave where my brother Abraham, dead at eighteen
months in the flu epidemic of 1919, was buried.

There was a pebble on the corner of the headstone
that had not been there two weeks earlier, so I knew that
either Mama or Papa had been to visit. All I had seen
was a faded snapshot of a beaming young Sophie and
Meyer holding an unidentifiable bundle, but to me Abraham had been growing up all the time I was. When I
visited his grave, it was to talk to my handsome older
brother. He would have friends to take me out, would be
giving my parents money so that I would not have to
work, would be helping me to decide what to do after
graduation.

The air turned chill, and the shadow of the headstone

lengthened. It was time to leave, for the sky darkened noticably earlier now than just a few weeks before. At home Mama's look told me she was disappointed that my afternoon out had not been spent with a suitable young man.

Chapter 2

Many times in the year since I had started to work, I wished that I could take back my words to Papa. I had not known, when I asked him to find me a job, how much I would hate my hours at the Smart Set. There my desk at the back was walled off from counters, boxes, and people by a partition; the lower half, dark-colored wood, the upper, glass etched in a pattern of leaves and vines. The only other employee was the "salesgirl," Mrs. Carter, who was not a girl, but a middle-aged widow with two children. When not helping customers, she stood at the counter in front of the stockings. At the cash register near the door sat Mr. Goldstein's wife. From there Mrs. Goldstein could watch the customers so that they would not steal anything, Mrs. Carter so that she delivered work for every penny of her salary, Mr. Goldstein so that he properly displayed each new item. I could see that she was also watching me. I did not know why, for I was cut off from anything I might steal. All I ever handled were numbers.

Then I realized Mrs. Goldstein thought I might be embezzling. I wanted to slam the ledger shut, run to the front of the store, and shout at her, "Stop looking at me. I don't know how to embezzle. Miss Brigham didn't teach that in Bookkeeping One. Maybe she will in Bookkeeping Two. You won't have to worry about me until I've learned a little more." I started to laugh as I pictured Mrs. Goldstein listening to all that; but I stopped when I thought that perhaps, after I had finished Bookkeeping Two, after I had graduated from high school, I might still be pinned behind glass in the Smart Set. I went back to the columns of figures, trying to shut out the image of working for years, maybe forever, under Mrs. Goldstein's roving, critical eye.

The Forgetown I knew was not the one my parents had come to as newlyweds. Then it had been prosperous, proud of the shops on Easton Street; the Iron Works that had been turning out cast-iron deer, fence sections, and curlicued gates for fifty years; and the Star-of-the-East mine, four miles outside of town, that produced a grade of iron ore much in demand by factories all along the East Coast.

Papa had come to the United States from Poland at seventeen and had spent eight years learning to be a tailor of ladies' clothing. Mama, born on Orchard Street on New York's Lower East Side, was orphaned at nine and raised by her cousins, the Ellenbogens. When it was time for her to marry, they had introduced her to Meyer Levine.

Many times while I was growing up, Mama had told me how Tanta Ellenbogen had shaken her head when she heard of Meyer's decision to settle in Forgetown. Clicking her false teeth, Tanta had said, "You'll live, you'll die, all the time with *goyim*. You'll see, Sophie, you'll see." But Tanta had been wrong. Sophie and Meyer found other Jews in Forgetown. Enough of them so that the Congregation Sons of Zion had, for sixteen years, been buying a building from the Farmers National Bank. There was seldom a morning when a *minyan*, the ten men necessary to conduct a service, did not meet at the *shul*. Occasionally, when someone was missing, an early-morning phone call might wake us all. Papa might be told that not only was he needed to be part of the ten, but that Samuel must hurry with him so that the service could begin.

On Easton Street at the river's edge, at the bottom of an inverted, tilted ⊤, stood the Forgetown Iron Works, owned by Edgar Wallington. An ornate fence, forged at the mill itself, enclosed the five buildings and the two brick smokestacks that dominated the town.

Mr. Wallington's wife had been one of the Jacksons, who owned the Star-of-the-East mine, most of the buildings on Easton Street, and the whole top of Broadway. There the Wallington's house, gabled and turreted, backed by a stand of maples, now stood, silhouetted against the sky.

Past the Works, on land that had been a cornfield off

Turning the Corner

Easton Street, was the cemetery where Abraham lay. Beyond the cemetery dairy farmers grazed their cows on the rich bottomland lining our side of the river.

Forgetown had been good to Papa at first. But then, in the winter of 1918–19, he did not open the store for the six weeks that he had been ill himself, nursed Mama, and buried his son. The first day he was well enough to go downtown, he discovered that the landlord had sold his furniture and the customers' clothes to cover the rent.

With a loan from Uncle Ellenbogen Papa had started again. Now the young man's certainty of success, which had carried him so far from his birthplace, was tempered by age but not stilled. He continued to make ladies' suits with beautifully bound buttonholes and hand-picked lapels, despite the hard times that had dried up the demand.

The trickle of money from Papa's customers was stretched and juggled to pay for our food, clothes, and rent for a house—sadly needing paint—on Monroe Street, unfashionably close to Easton, where empty stores were black marks among the still-open shops.

Although Forgetown had weathered the Stock Market Crash, Black Tuesday, of 1929, it had been badly hurt by the closing of the Star-of-the-East two years later. That winter an endless stream of men drifted back and forth on Easton Street—leather-jacketed, unshaven, blinking in the sunlight, looking for work. We were used to hoboes, men who had hopped on a freight train in a town that had offered no work and who had found themselves, many miles later, in Forgetown, the end of a branch line. Mama always had a sandwich of the previous night's meat loaf, or a scrambled egg, or a bit of leftover stew meat for those vagrants who knocked at her kitchen door. But after the mine shut down, some of them were men who had lived in Forgetown all their lives.

Gradually they had disappeared from the streets. I wondered if they hid in run-down row houses at the end of Easton Street, having no reason to leave. Or were they on the road, seeking work, any work; no more strange in faraway towns than in Forgetown, where daylight had been saved for women and children and their lives ran out when the vein did.

Then, after the Bank Holiday in 1933, the Forgetown Savings Bank did not reopen. On Easton Street, once busy stores failed. Boards were nailed over windows that had formerly been cleaned and polished to show off dishes and clothes, dry goods and furniture. These boards, in turn, were hidden by handbills and advertisements that after the first winter became unsightly streamers, torn loose by the rains to fill the gutters.

Since Halloween, Forgetown had been preparing for winter. Prudent homeowners had wrapped their shrubs in burlap. Glass-and-wood storm porches reappeared, protecting the front doors of the Wallingtons' house and those of a few others near the top of Broadway. Friday, the twenty-second of November, Janet and I started our day as usual at the corner of Broadway and Cross Street. In school we separated to go to our lockers, having decided to spend Saturday night at my house. At the doorsill of Miss Robinson's class we met again. Janet, who had left me smiling, faced me now in a way that seemed suddenly grown-up and unbearably sad.

"Rebecca," she said. "It's awful. The Works failed."

"Shut down completely?" I thought of Mr. Somerset.

"I think so. Bobby Ragle just told me that the gates are bolted, and there's a sign up telling all employees to go home. They won't get paid until next Wednesday."

"Does that mean your father?" Janet shrugged but did not answer. "Has business been bad?" I asked.

"I don't know. Daddy always says"—here she spoke slowly, mimicking his drawl—" 'a gentleman, especially one from Macon, doesn't talk business when there are ladies present.' " In her normal voice she added, "And Mommy and I are always there. So he never says anything about the Works."

Miss Robinson rapped for attention with the end of her yardstick on the top of her desk. "*Asseyez-vous!*" she commanded. "*Parlez seulement français. Il faut que nous étudiions la leçon.*"

My classmates, stunned by the news, clung together near the door, as if for mutual support, spreading out down the rows only after repeated desktop rapping. We looked for comfort in the established routine, in the familiarity of our alphabetically assigned seats. As I shuffled my books and papers I willed myself to believe that the brick chimneys still spewed out plumes of black smoke and that on this day, as on every other I could remember, the steam whistle would announce at noon that it was time for lunch, and at five thirty, that I could soon leave work. There must have been no whistle in the morning. It was strange we hadn't noticed, for it usually blew just as Heshie walked through the door looking for Samuel.

I wondered how much Forgetown would be changed by this new catastrophe. Now the men whose lives had been shaped by the hours they spent at the Works faced a world where they, too, had nothing to do. I pictured Mr. Wallington, gray-haired, well-tailored and -fed, moving about in a building where all else was stilled. Then I realized what the closing might mean to us if Mrs. Wallington could no longer afford to have Papa make suits for her.

He might have to find a still cheaper shop on a second story or a half basement on the edges of Easton Street. We might all need my salary so much that I would have to leave high school without graduating to work full-time at the Smart Set.

French class seemed to last for hours. The classes that followed it dragged on so, that by the time the day had ended, it seemed as though we had lived through a week since breakfast. As I walked despondently out of the building, Heshie caught up to me. "Don't look so sad, Rebecca. It'll work out, I'll bet you." He was so earnest, trying to cheer me up, that I could not help smiling.

Janet walked with me to the Smart Set, both of us thinking more than talking. At the door I left her to hurry to my desk at the back. I hung my sweater on the hook behind my desk and pulled the big ledger toward me to start where I had left off the day before.

Chapter 3

As winter settled in to stay I thought Forgetown seemed little changed despite the closing of the Works. I said so to Samuel as we walked up the hill one evening to supper.

"Nothing changes in this town," he said. "Nothing happens." He stopped at the foot of the concrete steps that climbed our steep front lawn. He was nearly six feet tall, his brown hair curly but more manageable than mine, his brown eyes shining now as he spoke. "In New York, or Chicago, or Hollywood, there's excitement. People have money to do things, go places. The Grand Canyon, the beach at Waikiki, Paris . . . the whole world. And no one here cares that they'll never see any-place else. They don't even want to *hear* about places that are far away. Sometimes—I never told anyone this, not even Heshie, no one—sometimes it's like there's someone out there calling me. 'Samuel Levine,' I hear, 'it's waiting. Anything you want. Just come and get it.' "

It was February, and in my winter coat I was cold as I listened. But Samuel's forehead was glazed faintly with perspiration that, I realized, came with the excitement of merely talking of places he hoped one day to see.

Two nights later, at the dinner table, he pulled a note out of his pocket and without speaking handed it to Mama. It was similar to one that had come earlier from Miss Robinson.

"Another command performance," Mama said when she finished reading. "What subject is Mrs. Addams?"

"Geometry," Samuel mumbled.

"Three fifteen tomorrow in Room One-oh-five she wants me."

"Should I tell her you'll be there?"

"Of course I'll be there. I know that school is important, even if you don't."

Dinner after the conference was inedible. Mama did not get home until nearly five, for the principal had stopped in to add his comments to those of Mrs. Addams. Samuel's teachers all agreed, he had told Mama, that Samuel was bright and imaginative, but all said he seemed unwilling to spend the necessary time and effort to get good grades. In the hour before dinner Mama could not make one of her long-simmering stews with glistening brown gravy over a boiled potato that broke apart with a rush of steam at the touch of my fork. To Mama's disappointment at the poor report about her son was added chagrin that she had to feed her family hamburgers, to her the symbol of a lazy housewife.

Samuel had obvious trouble swallowing his food, while I, watching with embarrassment, found that nothing tasted right to me either. Mama, her plate pushed aside, repeated the familiar words about the need to do well in school.

On this night, Mama's words rang in my ears like the sound of nails being hammered into the door of my office in the Smart Set, locking me there for good. If Samuel did not do well in school so that he could get a good job and help out at home, I might never be able to leave scowling Mrs. Goldstein and the rows of figures in my ledger.

Since the Works had closed, I could tell that my parents were worried about money, but in spite of my weekly contribution, I was treated like a child about the family finances. One night, however, I heard them through the wall between our bedrooms. Mama had been humiliated by the butcher. "You," she said. "You can be a big shot and not ask Mrs. Miller for money because her husband is out of work." Her voice shrilled as she warmed to her grievances. "Fine for Mrs. Miller. But what about your family? What do you care that the butcher tells me not to come again until I can pay?"

"Shush, Sophie, shush. Rebecca is right next door."

"So let Rebecca hear. Doesn't she know already what trouble it is to put food on the table with what you give me? Doesn't she know she hasn't had a new dress in three years? That my shoes are so old that no matter how hard I polish, I can't get a shine?"

I burrowed under my quilt to escape the sound of her voice. I wanted to tell my mother not to scold my father, that it was not his fault that people wanted cheap machine-made goods instead of his beautiful handmade clothes. I did not want him to become one who grabbed pennies, like Mr. Greenspan, even from the poorest and the sickest. Tears rolled down my cheeks and collected in the cups made by my collarbone as I hugged my knees. Mama's complaints, I thought, just made everything worse, since, when so much was wrong, all we had was each other.

I was awake for hours after the voices stopped, fearful of a month when we might not have the thirty-seven dollars for the landlord. I imagined my family on the sidewalk at night, in the cold, walled around by the wine-colored mohair sofa, its worn spots shining in the streetlight, the armchairs up-ended on top of each other. There would be Mama crying on a kitchen chair; me hiding between the china cabinet and the buffet from the onlookers who would come with the daylight; Papa and Samuel turning away in shame that they had not been able to prevent our trouble.

It had not been too different in 1933, when the Thompsons down the street at Number Fifteen had lost their house. Mr. Thompson had been treasurer of the Forgetown Savings Bank. Mr. and Mrs. Thompson and their five children had lived in the nicest house on our block. Papa explained to us then about mortgages. Most people need to borrow money when they buy a house, he had said. The borrowers have the option, if they cannot keep up payments on the principal, of paying only the interest. Mr. Thompson had lost some money in the Crash, the rest when the bank did not reopen after the Bank Holiday. When he no longer had even his salary and the mortgage came due, he could not pay or renegotiate his loan, so his family was dispossessed. All their belongings were piled on the street, guarded by the family until Mr. Thompson's brother came with his truck to cart their things to the barn on his farm. Our neighbors the Thompsons moved in with the other Thompsons, although everyone knew there wasn't room for both families.

But however crowded it would be, the Thompsons had a house to go to when they lost their own. Not so the hoboes who called at our kitchen door looking for food. I knew how some of them lived. Because my father owned a secondhand De Soto, we were able to visit relatives or, in the summer, to drive occasionally to the seashore. Sometimes we saw more than we had planned. Near the airport at Newark, New Jersey, there was a Hooverville: a village of shanties built of old boxes, of tin cans hammered flat, of parts of billboards whose faces still bore tattered remnants of signs. Hundreds of these shacks, a few with a thin line of smoke rising from tall tin cans that served as chimneys, were set down on acres of hardened mud. No blade of grass, no growing thing, was to be seen anywhere. In front of some of the shacks one, two, or three men sat, sometimes around a small fire over which, on an improvised tripod, another tin can hung. I could imagine nothing worse than living on such a barren field.

Such were the fears that lengthened my nights. But days were easier to get through. I was busy with school, with my job. After dinner I could not sit gossiping with Pa over tea. I was doubling up to do both commercial and college preparatory courses, so I always had an assignment to finish. Most days ended with the careful washing of my white sharkskin collar and cuffs, which had to be rubbed hard enough to get out the grime, but not so roughly that they would wear out. Some nights I wanted to tear the fabric to shreds so that I would have to replace them even though I would have a hard time finding money for new ones.

The Saturdays and Sundays of my senior year were chasing each other across the calendar. Some Saturday nights Janet and I, joined occasionally by Marcia Feldman, who was also a senior, speculated about what our classmates would do with the rest of their lives. We sat and talked late into the night, fitting together bits of news like a giant jigsaw puzzle whose pieces were real people.

In school the halls bore evidence of spring as sure as the first robins. Notices appeared about tryouts for the senior play, and requests for volunteers for committees for the Senior Prom. But I was no closer now than I had been in September to finding a date for the dance.

I did not talk about it at home, but Samuel, who had also seen the signs, must have guessed what was on my mind. One March night as we walked home from a Tyrone Power movie, without Heshie, who was visiting relatives, Samuel said, "Boy, you'd knock those other senior girls right off their rockers if you brought someone who looked like him to the dance."

"I'd settle for someone who looked like Charlie Chaplin."

"There's not much choice in this dumb place."

"I know." I had sorted through the school, homeroom by homeroom, to make sure I missed no one. I was one of the tallest senior girls, and I wanted to dance with a boy whose eyes I could see.

"Why don't you ask Heshie? He's tall, and he likes you. He says you're one of the prettiest girls in town."

I smiled, picturing Heshie: big, fair-haired, with large hands and feet—three of each, it always seemed, because he had so much trouble knowing what to do with them when he talked. I stopped smiling. "I can't take a sopho-more. Everyone would know I couldn't get anyone else."

"I have an idea. The weekend of the dance we'll stay at Tanta Greenbaum's, and I'll take you to Radio City Music Hall."

"I bet if someone broke a leg, you'd suggest a movie to make it better." I could have hugged Samuel to thank him for trying to help but instead I straightened his jacket where it had bunched up in back from being sat on in the Plaza. Not even the opera, if it had been of-fered, I thought, could make up for not having a date for my Senior Prom, but I couldn't tell that to my brother.

On the way to school the following Friday, I suggested to Janet we meet at my house the next night. I had not been invited to the Somersets for a long time and could not understand why. I knew that her mother liked me, and with Mr. Somerset in Panama, I thought that a visi-tor, even though it would be only me, would still be a change for Janet and her mother.

"I don't like coming to your house all the time when I can't ask you to mine."

"What difference does it make whose house we're at?"

"It does to me. But I can't help it. It's Daddy. He hasn't been out of the house since the Works closed."

"But I thought he was away on a job."

"That's what he told us to say. But it's not true. Nobody offered him a job after the Works closed. He doesn't even bother to get dressed anymore. Just sits all day in his pajamas and bathrobe. To save his clothes, he says. If he goes out, the pavements will wear down his soles."

"But the Works closed in November, and now it's March. What does he do all day?"

"Oh, Rebecca." Janet closed her eyes for a minute as though visualizing her father at home. "He sits. In the kitchen. He won't sit in the living room with their bed and dresser down there. If he hears a noise on the porch, he hides."

I remembered Mr. Somerset, who always came to dinner in a suit with a vest. He looked as if, before coming downstairs, he had bathed and shaved and changed all his clothes. Now, I thought, he must be like an old man, in wrinkled nightclothes, his breath bad, his face unshaven.

"Your parents sleep downstairs?"

"We all do. We shut off the upstairs radiators to save heat, and it's like Siberia up there. I sleep in the kitchen on an army cot that I fold up in the morning. We don't even go upstairs to the bathroom but just sponge ourselves in the downstairs washroom. I haven't had a real bath since before Christmas. I wonder what will happen if soap gets too expensive."

"Why didn't you say something sooner? Tell your mother I want you to sleep over tomorrow night. Then you can take a long hot bath."

"Oh, Rebecca, that would be wonderful. Are you sure it will be all right? I won't stay for breakfast."

"Don't worry about breakfast. Papa made a suit for Mrs. Dietrich out at the farm. She told him they got so little for their milk and eggs that she had no money for him. So Papa said to bring us milk and eggs whenever they had extra until he was paid. Now every week, Mr. Dietrich brings a crate of eggs and a big jug of milk. Mama is good at making eggs, so you hardly know you're eating them."

"Eggs must be cheap, we eat them a lot. And beans and spaghetti." I nodded, but didn't say anything, for it seemed to me that Janet had more to say. "Every Monday morning Mommy walks to the bank and takes out ten dollars. That has to pay for everything for the whole week."

Now I stopped her. "I thought a law was just passed to give people money when they lost their jobs."

"It was. But it doesn't help anybody who lost a job before. If my daddy were working now, and then lost his job, he'd be entitled to some money. But as it is, we only have what he saved."

"I know it sounds dreadful. But what about Home Relief? My father says that the government has an obligation to help people when times are hard."

"My father would starve first, I do believe. Mommy once said something about it to him, and he said she must think that he isn't man enough to keep his family off the dole. It upset him so much, Mommy and I know now we can never mention it again."

"But is there enough in the bank?"

"I don't even know that. She won't tell me. I know we lost some when the Forgetown Savings Bank failed. . . ."

"Bank Holiday. How could they call that a holiday?" I remembered February and March of 1933, our sophomore year, in the weeks before Franklin D. Roosevelt's inauguration. Almost every bank in the country had been closed by the governors of the states, so they wouldn't fail. As soon as Roosevelt was President he declared a national four-day Bank Holiday while Congress passed new laws regulating banks and protecting depositors. As soon as the law was signed sound banks reopened. The Forgetown Savings Bank on Easton Street, next to the Smart Set, was one of the ones that didn't. I knew that many people had lost savings, but not that the Somersets had been among them.

Janet must have been remembering those times too. "I think that Daddy always planned that I would marry Mr. Stanton's son, Frederick junior. Nobody blamed Mr. Stanton when the bank failed. Everyone knew he was an honorable man. Just that his friends talked him into taking worthless properties as security. No one has heard from the Stantons since they moved away."

"I feel so dumb. You've had all this trouble, and I never guessed." I was ashamed of the hours I had spent worrying about the dance when Janet had serious problems on her mind.

"I was too embarrassed to say anything. But today I

thought I would burst if I didn't talk to someone. I don't know what will happen if one of us gets sick. I've stopped eating candy altogether, because I know if I get a toothache, there's just no money for a dentist."

"And I went right on picturing everything the way it used to be. That you ate in the dining room every night—"

"Oh, we still do. Only now the chairs are turned so we don't see the bed in the living room. And Mommy and I try not to notice that Daddy is wearing his bathrobe. . . . Thank you, Rebecca, for listening to all this."

When something bothered me, I could talk to Samuel, or to Abraham. But Janet had only a sister ten years older, married and living in Arizona. Margaret's husband, I had been told, had never been able to earn enough money to move his wife and daughter out of his parents' house. A visit home from Margaret seemed a near impossibility. I was glad I had been able to help my friend by listening to her. Selfishly, however, I felt cheated. I had lost a pleasant, comfortable house that until now I had been able to escape to in my imagination.

Later, walking home past the boarded-up stores, I wondered what chance Janet and I had of becoming anything except cranky old salesladies or bookkeepers. Our town seemed to contract each day, the dead parts eating up the live ones. Soon all that was fresh and full of juice would be sucked dry. I wrapped my old maroon coat around me more tightly, as though it would protect me, would keep my skin fresh and full, my eyes bright, my hopes alive.

Whenever I walked on Easton Street, I turned my face away from the Works. The winter seemed to have done its worst there. The yard had collected windborne flotsam. Newspapers tossed by the north and west winds were trapped by the fence and spilled in an arc from the southeast corner. Unhappiness and trouble seemed to be spreading up from the Works to engulf the few remaining pleasant places in Forgetown.

Chapter 4

The winter winds that had nightly driven me home to dinner gradually lessened. While we could not yet say spring was here, we could no longer deny that it would be soon. On the last Wednesday in March my family was already at dinner when I got home. Mama had served the meal a half hour earlier than usual, for Papa wanted to attend the meeting of the Wainford County Socialist Party, of which he was a charter member.

At ten thirty he came home, calling to Mama and Samuel from the hallway. "Come to the dining room, where Rebecca is," he said, motioning toward the table, where I was doing my homework, my books and papers fanned out in front of me.

"Ed Feldman and Marty Grogan want me to run for sheriff."

"Sheriff?" Mama asked. "Who ever heard of a Jewish sheriff?"

"With a big hat and gun, Pa?" Samuel wanted to know.

"You watch too many cowboy movies. Here in the East, sheriffs are supposed to evict people who don't pay rent."

"But, Papa, how could you evict anyone? What if it were winter? Or they were sick?" Here was my nightmare turned inside out.

"About that you don't have to worry," he answered. "Never could I do such a thing. Besides, you think Wainford County would ever elect a *Socialist*?" We shook our heads. "The committee wants a complete Socialist slate. They think Norman Thomas will have a better chance that way."

"But, Meyer," Mama protested, "running for office is a rich man's business."

"Ed and Marty know I'm not rich. They'll take care of expenses. Not that it'll be so much. A few dollars for signs to put up."

The discussion did not end there. That night as I lay in bed, Mama continued. "How can you think you won't have to spend? It has to cost money. Money we don't have."

"If we don't have, then I can't spend, Sophie. We'll manage. This way I feel that I'm doing something. That maybe things will change."

"Dreams," Mama said. "All the time dreams. Dreams don't buy meat."

"We never went without yet. And we won't now."

How could Papa sound so sure, I wondered, when everything was wearing out and nothing being replaced. Except his dreams. They were young and fresh. Maybe I was the one who was old, with an old woman's ideas, while Papa was young—in his dreams at least. He could listen to Mama grumble at night and in the morning still go down to open the store, where there might be no work. I was truly young, I was strong; maybe *I* was getting things turned around. I should be able to hold on tight, even if it seemed as though Forgetown was slipping down the hill into the river.

On the Sunday following Papa's announcement, the first sunny day after two cold weeks of rain, I went out to the cemetery to tell Abraham about the office our father might hold. "Can you imagine—our Papa, a sheriff? Election day, we'll all have new clothes, and Papa will make a speech to thank Ed Feldman, and the Grogans, and old Mrs. Morris when they congratulate him."

Then the wind changed, telling me it was still March. I hurried home to find my parents discussing the logistics of our trip to the Ellenbogens for the Passover Seder. Samuel and I always looked forward to these visits, for we seldom saw our cousins. One hundred miles of uncertain transportation lay between us. This year we would have to travel three hours by train to New York City and a half hour more by subway to get there. But we would be rewarded, not only by a party with Tanta's good food, but by a chance to measure our life against that of our city cousins. We were fascinated to hear them tell how they and their friends would escort each other— whole apartment houses full of friends—to *shul* on Rosh

Hashanah and Yom Kippur, just as they walked to school on ordinary days. In Forgetown on Jewish holidays I could not shake the feeling that something was wrong, that I did not belong, dressed up and home from school, while all about me life went on in its usual weekday patterns.

This year the train and subway made more stops than I remembered. I was afraid we would be late and would spoil the dinner. The Ellenbogens lived in six rooms on two floors above their store. The rich scent of roasting chickens and browned onions, the moist odor of chicken soup sweetened with carrots, the dry lemony smell of the matzo meal sponge cake, the vapors of caramelized stewed apples, welcomed us despite our lateness.

Tanta's kitchen was in the back of the second floor. In front the living room overlooked the street, but both could be reached only through the windowless dining room with its long table covered in endless white. Tanta's Passover dishes were also white with a narrow gold rim enclosing scattered rosebuds. I always marveled that anyone could have so many matching dishes that would be used for only one week a year. But when I thought that they had already seen service at Seders for forty years, owning them seemed less extravagant.

Our arrival was greeted with ritual exclamations about how much we had grown. Before, I had always heard these words with embarrassment. For though I had not grown since I was fifteen, I had towered over my boy cousins since I was eleven. This year they had caught up. It seemed impossible that it could have happened, but there was cousin Maxel, smiling *down* on me.

"Well, Rebecca. Still the best student in Forgetown?"

"Second best," Samuel answered, not without pride, I thought. "She's salutatorian, not valedictorian."

"Not bad for a girl," Maxel said. "And a hick, at that."

"Now, Maxel," Tanta interrupted, "don't be fresh. Rebecca's your guest."

"It's all right. She knows I'm joking."

I hadn't and had begun to bristle, but when I saw Maxel smile, I realized that this was his way of paying attention and I would spoil the evening if I acted hurt. Soon we were all at the long table: Maxel and his brother, Saulie; Samuel and me; and the four cousins from the other side, all of us sitting as far as we could from the head of the table, where Uncle and Papa and the other old men droned on with the service. We talked and winked and giggled across to each other, while from the end of the table an angry *"Shah, kinder"* would silence us for a few minutes.

Under cover of the passing plates laden with aromatic food, I watched Maxel. I saw him lean over the Haggadah, the prayer book for the Seder service, his brown hair curling over the edge of his prayer cap. My body seemed to be sending peculiar messages. My fingers and toes were calling attention to themselves with a new insistence. I felt as if my blood were pumping at new speeds to new places. Heated from the warmth between my legs, faster than its normal rate, it pushed to my face and ears, making them blush and pale with each beat and retreat.

When no one was watching, I leaned close to Samuel

with an important question. "Do you think I could ask Maxel to the dance? I'd die if he said no."

"He won't say no."

"How can you tell?"

"It's a feeling I have. And besides, if he does say no," added the ever practical Samuel, "he won't say he doesn't like you. He'll think of some excuse so you won't feel bad."

"But it's so far."

"If he wants to come, it won't be far."

After eating more than I thought possible and plowing sleepily through the end of the service, drugged by the unaccustomed wine, I finally had a chance to speak to Maxel.

"I wonder, before I go. . . . On June twentieth, a Saturday, we're having a dance. In the gym. I know it's far, but could you come?"

"It's a weekend, so if Cousin Sophie would let me stay over, I could." He smiled. I saw that Samuel had been right. Maxel didn't think it would be too far.

"Of course you can stay." Maxel and I stood close together, apart from the others. There was more that had to be said. I had rehearsed it all through tea and dessert. "The class voted to pay for the dance with profits from the senior play. And we decided no corsages, because of the Depression." I could feel the red come and go in my face as I talked. As soon as I finished I felt my normal color returning, and I smiled for the first time.

Maxel noticed. "You're pretty when you don't worry," he said. He wasn't smiling, though, and hesitated for a second over what might have been hard for him to say. "Could you do me a favor, Rebecca? When you introduce me, could you call me Max? Maxel is for babies. I try to tell them here—"

"Of course. Max is much nicer," I agreed. Now we both smiled with relief, and I hurried to my family, already halfway into their coats at the door. Samuel looked at me and whispered, "I'll bet he said yes." I nodded. "He can have my room if he wants. What else did he say?"

"He said to call him Max," I answered. Sleepily we headed for the subway, having resisted all invitations to stay overnight. Mama wanted to be home to prepare for our Seder on the second night, to which she had invited the Toplinskys and the Greenspans.

During the long train ride home, over the miles to the end of the line, riding as Papa did when he first visited Forgetown, I thought that in a few weeks Max would travel the same way and arrive, smiling and handsome, to take me to the dance. But before that could happen, I had something important to discuss with my father. I had saved five dollars by spending none of the twenty-five cents I kept back each week from my salary. With it Papa could buy material for a dress for me to wear. I knew he would not want to take my money, so had put off offering it. But now that I had a date for the dance, which was only eight weeks away, I could wait no longer. While Mama and Samuel dozed, I took the bill from my bag and handed it to him in the facing seat. "To buy material for a graduation dress."

Papa shook his head. "I don't need your money. What kind of a tailor would I be if I couldn't find material to make a dress for my daughter's graduation? I wanted to surprise you. But, now that you know, you should come for a fitting. Tomorrow morning before Mama gets busy with the cooking, we'll go to the shop."

I nodded and leaned my head against the seat. Now I, too, could sleep. I knew we had finally reached Forgetown when the conductor came through our car, flipping the backs of the empty seats. On the last train of the night, in the town at the end of the line, the seats had to be turned so they faced the other way for the first trip outward the following day.

Next morning, most of Easton Street was alive with Tuesday activity. Papa's shop, however, was closed for the holiday, the shades pulled on the large front window. From behind the curtain that separated the dressing room from the shop, he pulled out a dress on a hanger.

Papa watched my face anxiously. "I worked on it mornings only, so you shouldn't come by after school and maybe see."

"Oh, it's beautiful, Pa," I said, fingering the crisp organdy.

"The material is from Myra Pierson's wedding gown. A double train she wanted at first. Then she changed her mind and said a single. When I asked her did she want the extra material, she said no, she didn't sew. I didn't argue. There was extra lining too. That makes the slip."

The dress had a gathered skirt beneath a bodice of deep horizontal tucks. The round collar was edged with leaves embroidered in fine white silk. Where the rows of tucks met, Papa had hand stitched neat buttonholes. The buttons were mother-of-pearl daisies. Papa saw me looking at them and said, "Four, maybe five years ago, a customer wanted me to take these off and put on brass. Too old-fashioned, she said. I knew someday I would want daisies. When I came to make your dress, it was time."

I saw something blue on the hanger. "What's that?"

"I was waiting for you to ask. That sash you wear on the dress when you wear it to the dance. Other times, it has a plain belt to match." The sash was a long ribbon of pale blue taffeta. "Remember Celia Wallington's spring suit? This was the lining. I thought how good this color would be, and so I cut very carefully the lining." He fingered the sash. "It's pieced in six places, but believe me, an expert wouldn't know."

"Could I try it on?"

"And what did you think a fitting was?"

The dress had short puffed sleeves and a skirt that belled out as I twirled. I grimaced at my brown school shoes that tarnished the image of the fairy princess in the pier glass. Then I remembered. "The five dollars that you didn't need for the dress. That'll be for shoes."

"You see, maybe it's sometimes good to have a tailor for a father."

"No. It's good to have Meyer Levine for a father." I hugged Papa. Then, impatient, I stood as quietly as I could while he adjusted the placket and marked the hem. Instead of standing in Papa's shop, I wanted to run out into the early spring morning to announce that I was going to the dance after all, in a new dress, with Max at my side. I wished that Sunday would come quickly so that I could tell Abraham of my good fortune. I wondered if I could bring Max to meet my secret ally, or if he would think me peculiar when he learned of my visits to the cemetery.

Chapter 5

For the rest of the school year my days were colored by the feelings that came with the sound of Max's name. Each morning, as I walked down our hill, a Rebecca I didn't know seemed to pull at my sweater and say of school, "Don't go into those stuffy halls. Stay out here with the young grass and the spring sun. Winter is over at last." But the familiar Rebecca led me instead to meet Janet on Broadway each morning.

"You're the only one I can tell," she said one day, "because you know about my father. He won't come to my graduation because he's supposed to be in Panama. . . ."

"Can't he come home sometimes?"

"He says everyone will see how pale he is and know

that he never went away. Rebecca, nothing is going to make him come out of that house until he gets a job. And how can he if he just sits there? The phone is gone now, so no one could call him even if they wanted to."

"Once you're working, you can have it put back." The music that had played in my head since Max had told me that he would come to the dance had stopped. Now a sound echoed there that I recognized as the clang of the last closing of the Works' gates. Graduation night, which should be joyous for Janet, would be bitter, instead, without her father there. Ashamed, I realized that I wanted to cheer Janet up not merely for her sake, but so that my happiness would not be dimmed.

"It's still more than two weeks away. Maybe your father will change his mind."

She shook her head. "You don't know what this has done to him. He won't."

I had been thinking of ways I might help Janet. "Come for dinner," I said. "Maybe we can figure something out." We were in front of the school now, and all I was able to offer was a change of scene for an evening.

"I don't like to leave Mommy and Daddy. They wait for me to come with the news. . . . But maybe this once."

Later I called Mama from the Smart Set to tell her that things were not going well at the Somersets and that I had invited Janet to dinner. I asked her to please put an extra potato in the stew, and promised I would eat carefully so that there would be enough.

I knew that she understood when I saw that we would not be eating, as we usually did, on the white enamel kitchen table with the leaves pulled up. Instead, Mama had set the dining room table with an ivory-colored cloth, its edges banded in blue, its center decorated with scattered flowers that looked like blue violets. Mama, Samuel, Janet, and I were all in our chairs facing the large platter from Mama's *flayshig* dinner set, the dishes we used for meat. Tonight the platter held a stew of small cubes of beef, large carrot slices, and halves of browned potatoes, all in a wonderfully fragrant gravy. Papa called down the stairs that we should start without him and that he would be right down.

Mama was ladling out the stew when a noise in the hallway made us all turn. Just emerging from one side of the archway was the head of a pirate. I recognized my red bandanna and a gold hoop-earring that was one of a pair from Tanta Ellenbogen that Mama had thought too garish to wear, but too good to discard. Papa had blacked out several teeth and streaked his cheeks with charcoal. Even Mama had to laugh.

We ate dinner, Papa still a pirate from the neck up, but from there down, Meyer Levine in gray herringbone trousers and a dark gray cardigan. We giggled all through the meal. Afterward over tea Papa, growing serious, said, "We laugh, but maybe this is how I should dress when I talk to people about the election. Big business is nothing but pirates, stealing all the time from the working man. Only Norman Thomas has plans to protect him from exploitation."

I was grateful that both my parents had tried to make the evening pleasant for Janet, but before nine I was walking her partway home so both of us could finish our homework. Under the trees now in full leaf we agreed it was impossible to believe that in two weeks we would walk together to Forgetown High School for the last time.

The ten days between the end of classes and the weekend of the prom were endless. Finally Saturday came. I scrubbed up in the washroom next to my office in the Smart Set, changed into my prom dress, and hurried to the station to meet Max's train. He was even more handsome than I remembered. I could see that he knew the dance was important, for he was wearing a good blue suit. Together we battled the strangeness between us that had finally begun to dissolve at the Seder. Max made me laugh as he described the people who had traveled with him on his way to Forgetown.

As Max and I entered Forgetown High, I was assaulted by a gymnasium smell of aged sneakers and perspiration-soaked tumbling mats that I had never noticed when I was there every day. I looked carefully at all the other girls: Janet, Marcia, Edna Toplinsky, and the others. No one was wearing a dress as nice as my organdy. The daisy buttons shone. The pale blue taffeta sash was tied in a big bow to call attention to my small waist, of which I was proud even when I felt ugly. I danced a hesitant two-step in the crepe-paper-trimmed room. I remembered that Max had said I was pretty when I smiled, and as he held me I smiled, inside and out. My feet even began to find a way of moving that seemed right.

I was sure that Max was the best-looking boy in the room. Not Frank Patterson and Buddy Grogan, who played football, nor any of the seniors I had once wished would ask me out, had a smile that my mouth answered automatically. From the way the other girls watched Max dance, I could tell that *they* thought him good-looking too. I had forgotten "cousin Maxel" as soon as Max had said he would come to the dance. My little cousin had grown into a tall young stranger who whirled me around the dance floor. I never once, even when I was flustered about who gets introduced to whom, forgot to call him Max.

As we were walking along Easton Street on our way home, Max held my hand and told me of his plans for September, when he would start at City College. "Maybe you'll come to one of my dances," he added.

"September seems so far away when the summer hasn't even started," I said hesitantly. The evening had turned cool. I didn't have a coat pretty enough to wear over my dress, so I had gone bare-armed to the dance. Max saw me shiver and stopped. Without saying anything, he took off his jacket and dropped it on my shoulders. I started to shake my head, but he began walking again, and I had to run to catch up.

"I'm still warm from the dancing," he insisted. "I don't need it."

I moved my shoulders under the padded shoulders of his jacket, enjoying the warmth of his body that the coat still held. At the house Max moved to the glider on the end of the porch. We sat rocking silently. He picked up my hand and began to stroke my palm. The tingling toes and fingers that his smile created wanted to dance at his touch. He was going to kiss me. Just then we heard a sound on the other side of the front door. It was opened by Mama in her nightgown and bathrobe. "I couldn't sleep so I came down to make myself some tea. Come in, I'll find some cookies, and you'll tell me about the dance."

To me it looked as though she hadn't tried to sleep at all, but had sat in the darkened room above the porch waiting for our return. Max and I followed her into the kitchen. My cheeks were red, I was sure, and my heart pounding from that second when Max had started to pull me toward him. Sometime before he left tomorrow, we would find another chance for him to kiss me.

Long after we were all in our own rooms, I lay awake. My head was filled with the clarinet solo from "Bill," and the soft shuffle of feet following the rhythm on a polished floor. "He's just my Bill, an ordinary guy . . ." Stage front, Max and I danced, twirling and dipping, my skirt and sash repeating my turns in graceful arcs. As we danced the background dissolved. The music swelled, we swung apart and together in a darkened room above a lighted cobweb of city streets; another crescendo and we whirled onto a marble pavilion thrust out above a motionless lake. Now the season changed, and we glided on ice skates before admiring onlookers on a mountaintop pond, my short skirt flaring straight out with each pirouette.

I giggled to see that with each sequence, Max and I were getting older, and I thought that next we might be followed out onto the floor by a graduated string of curly-haired boys and frizzy-haired girls high-kicking across the stage. A cough on the other side of the wall reminded me that my family was trying to sleep in the rooms all around mine. I forced myself to be quiet, and as night finally departed I drifted off to sleep.

We woke to bright sunshine enfolding the promise of a special day. After breakfast I decided to take Max to meet Abraham. I detoured around the intersection of Broadway and Easton to avoid the empty stores and the decaying Works, and we walked instead through streets that still presented ordered lawns and fresh paint. Soon the distances between the houses grew into fields covered with the green down of young corn, and finally to the one marked off by a stone wall that was the Jewish cemetery. I showed Max Abraham's grave but did not tell him that I often came to confide in the dead baby brother who had grown up to be my friend.

"You're right, it's pretty here," he said. "When you first talked about the cemetery, I thought it was spooky, but it's okay. Let's sit up there." He led me away from Abraham's grave to the big oak at the top of the rise. Before I could sit down, he pulled me toward him for the long-postponed kiss. His lips tasted of Mama's strawberry jam, which we had eaten for breakfast. My blood, which had seemed to stand still as he reached for me, began to pound back at double speed to where it belonged. I could tell Max liked it too. I curled my fingers in his hair and wanted to call him Maxel, but it was late, and time to leave for the station, if he was to make his train. Long after it had gone, I watched the track, seeing Max's curly brown head and his arm waving good-bye.

Graduation was Monday evening at seven thirty. This time I wore the matching tailored belt with my white dress. The crepe paper was gone from the gym and rows of folding chairs covered the dance floor, but the sense of my success on the night of the dance remained. Mama, Papa, and Samuel watched proudly from the fifth row as my name was announced as salutatorian.

My happiness was muted when I saw Mrs. Somerset sitting alone as Janet stepped up to accept the prize from the American Legion essay contest. I was sad for all the Somersets, but I hoped that Janet would be able at least to buy something for herself with the ten dollars she had won. Nothing would make up for not having her father there when she got the prize, but buying something might distract her from the memory of her pain.

This was the end of high school, but for me at least it was not a commencement of anything, but merely the continuation of dullness all around.

Chapter 6

As soon as school ended, Heshie and Samuel announced their plans to go into business. Mr. Greenspan had lent them money to buy two lawn mowers. Each morning, as I left for the Smart Set, they tried a different section of town. Each night when they counted up the day's receipts, they put some money aside to repay Mr. Greenspan. If it rained, they stayed at home and prepared Socialist Party election circulars for mailing to the voters.

After work and on weekends I, too, helped with the stack of leaflets in the front hall. That whole summer, while Papa canvassed the county in his old De Soto, the rest of us folded and stuffed an endless procession of pages analyzing the country's economic problems and setting forth the Socialists' proposed solutions.

One night, the last batch finished, Samuel and I were pushing ourselves in the glider to cool off, as Papa drove up. "Mama in bed?" he asked.

"I don't think so," I was saying, when Mama, in response to the slam of the car door, came out to the porch. "Would you like some iced tea? Meyer? Children?"

"First listen to what's happening!" Papa settled himself on the glider between Samuel and me. Mama sat on the chair from the hall that we moved to the porch at the beginning of each summer. "On September twenty-ninth Mr. Norman Thomas is coming here—to Forgetown."

"You're joking," I said.

"Absolutely not. He is coming in the flesh, in person. And to introduce him—guess who?"

"Meyer Levine, distinguished candidate for sheriff," said Samuel with a flourish. When Papa smiled and nodded, he added, "Wait till I tell Heshie."

"You had better tell more people than Heshie," Mama said. "If you want a crowd to hear him, you'll have to tell everyone you know."

"But, Ma, Norman Thomas is running for President of the whole United States," I said.

"Yeah," said Samuel. "Catch Roosevelt or Landon coming to a hick town like this."

"Where will he speak?" asked Mama.

"That we don't know for sure. Just now at the meeting of the executive committee, they told me to rent the American Legion Hall. It's new and it's comfortable. In the morning, first thing, I'll see Franklin Whyte."

We were not surprised that Papa was chosen to rent the hall. He was almost as good a candidate for office, and general legman, as a man so rich that he need not worry about working at all. Papa was responsible only to himself for the hours he kept in his shop. Two years earlier in mechanical drawing class Samuel had lettered, on heavy cardboard attached to a strong loop of twine, BACK IN ONE HOUR—GOODS CAN BE PICKED UP IN BARBER SHOP NEXT DOOR. When Papa moved, Samuel had inked out BARBER SHOP and replaced it with BAKERY. Wherever Papa had his shop, he found neighbors who were ready to pay for his smiling face and sympathetic ear by keeping the made-over dresses or altered trousers that his customers might want in his absence.

The next afternoon, from behind my half-glass partition, I saw Papa walk into the Smart Set. I was not surprised for each day on my way back to the store from lunch at home, I dropped in at Papa's to say hello. If I did not have time to stop, Papa would hang out his sign and walk around to see me.

This day he looked worried and asked for Mr. Goldstein. "Who ever heard, Harry shouldn't be in the shop?" he asked.

"He's here, Pa. In the back unloading blouses. What's wrong?"

Then Papa told me of his morning. He had called on Franklin Whyte at City Hall. Mr. Whyte was the town engineer and newly elected commander of the American Legion post. He saw Papa at once, for Papa's shop with its glowing coal stove was a good place to hide from the cold on tours of the town's installations. Mr. Whyte motioned Papa to a chair.

"Meyer, it's nice to have you visit me for a change. Sorry I don't have coffee. Is the sewer on the corner backing up again?"

"No, they fixed it when you told them. This time I came about the hall. To rent, for the regular price, of course."

"For a lecture on tailoring? Or, I bet I know. Secretly all these years you have been studying the violin, and now you want to give a—what do you call it?—a recital."

Papa shook his head. "That might have been a good idea, but to tell you the truth, I didn't think of it. No, I want the hall for Norman Thomas. He is coming to speak on September twenty-ninth, and we expect a big crowd."

"Well, Meyer, I think I can be pretty sure I speak for the entire membership. Now, we have nothing against Mr. Thomas himself. But some of his friends don't smell so good to us. And I don't think our membership would like to have him in our hall. If you'd like, I can bring it up at the next meeting. But I have to tell you that if I don't recommend it, there won't be any action. The members go a lot by what I say."

"If you couldn't recommend it, I wouldn't want you to bring it up. We'll find someplace else."

"What about the room they just fixed up at the synagogue? It's a good size. I went through it when you people filed the permit to enlarge."

"Your hall would be better but if not, then it will be the synagogue. Good-bye, Frank. I'll be in the shop later if you want coffee."

Papa finished telling me of his interview as Mr. Goldstein walked into the office. A businessman who spent most of his waking hours in his store, he felt that Meyer Levine's habit of closing his shop unnecessarily was not only bad for Papa's business, but reflected ill on all businessmen. Mr. Goldstein's duties as president of the Congregation Sons of Zion apparently also authorized him to supervise the religious life of his friends.

"Meyer, you weren't in *shul* this morning."

"Now that Herman is better and comes again regular, I didn't think you needed me for the *minyan*."

"A man should come to *shul* whether he is the tenth man or the hundredth."

"Maybe so. But meanwhile I came to rent the *shul* for a meeting."

"What kind of meeting?"

"I need a hall for Norman Thomas to speak. Since the *shul* was enlarged—"

"I don't think we should use the *shul* for politics. Especially your kind. This is a small town. They don't like Socialists here. The rest of us Jews can't afford to have our customers think we're Reds."

"Norman Thomas is no revolutionary. He only says that life should be a little easier for the working man. Maybe I should speak to the other members? Ones who used to belong to unions and don't feel like you?"

"Speak to whoever you want. Only remember, we are just a few people. If we fight among ourselves, we could lose our *shul*. And everything else it's taken us so long to get."

"I know the *shul* is important to the old men. Don't worry, I won't start a fight." Papa turned to me. "Rebecca, I'll see you at home." His smile, though jaunty, lacked conviction.

At half past five Mrs. Goldstein and Mrs. Carter, having meals to attend to, left the Smart Set. Mr. Goldstein and I stayed the last half hour until closing to catch the dollars of any late passerby. Usually Papa came to escort me home, reciting—with frequent stops to act out details —the events of his day.

At six, however, Papa was not out front. He did not overtake me until I had turned the final corner into Monroe Street. He looked weary. "I'm sorry I didn't walk with you," he said. "I had a few things on my mind, nothing serious, and I didn't notice it was six o'clock."

"Oh, Pa, you're worried about the meeting. There must be someplace. How about the Presbyterian Church?"

"I went there right after I left Harry's. And after them the Methodists. They both said the same: Churches shouldn't mix in politics. That they wouldn't say to Mr. Landon, you can be sure."

"Where will you try next?"

"I don't know. But I can't go back to the committee and say no one will let Mr. Thomas speak."

Our kitchen was hot from the residue of the August sun on the roof and the cooking that Mama would not abandon, even at ninety degrees. With unspoken agreement, after dinner we moved out to the porch to discuss finding a hall. Papa and Mama and I sat on the glider,

Samuel swung the chair to sit facing us, his arms crossed along the back. Papa was silent, but Samuel said, "We need a system. Rebecca, you get a pencil and paper. We'll list all the halls we can think of. Then we can decide where to ask first."

"The drawer of the table in the hall," Mama said to me. "You'll find paper and pencil." Writing quickly, I was surprised that Samuel seemed to name more places than all the rest of us, and to know of their size and condition.

Papa began to brighten as he saw the list grow to more than a dozen. "Good, good. Thank you all for your very good ideas. First thing in the morning I'll go to Doctor Englander about one of the schools. If he says no, and to tell you the truth, I think he will, then," Papa consulted the list, "I'll see Walter Czlaky about the Polish-American Hall."

"And I'll go see what Heshie's doing," Samuel said, swinging his chair to its normal position, his role as chairman concluded.

"Don't be late," Mama called to him as he started down the steps. "Maybe it's cool enough to do the dishes," she added, standing up.

"And I could see a few people yet tonight," said Papa.

I sat alone, pushing the glider to speed the breeze against my face as I watched the peaceful circle of street and lawn and stairs carved out by the streetlamp. I thought then of the Somersets. Mr. Somerset would no more be able to leave his house to escape the heat than to see his daughter graduate. Janet and Mrs. Somerset would feel obliged to stay with him. I left the porch, the glider swinging rapidly behind in reaction to my exit. If my friend had to be stuck indoors, I guessed I could stand it too.

Mama, on her way upstairs, said she was going to take a cold bath and try to sleep. Later from the living room I thought I heard someone on the stairs up from the street. I convinced myself I was imagining it and went back to my book. Still later, when I heard footsteps on the sidewalk in front of our house, I decided it was time to look around.

At first I saw nothing extraordinary. The concrete steps from the bottom of the porch ended in a pale ribbon of slates. Tonight, however, the ribbon was embroidered with an unfamiliar pattern. I followed the steps down for a better look. Large letters worked in bright yellow chalk ran from edge to edge of the slates. From the steps the words were upside down, so that in order to read them I had to step over the slates. RED JEW RED RED JEW RED RED JEW RED. I had never noticed that there were exactly nine slate rectangles across the narrow front of our house. On the twenty-four risers of the concrete steps, neatly centered, E over E, the words were repeated from the sidewalk to the porch.

I knew I would have to erase these terrible words before my parents saw them. As I entered the house Mama heard me. "Rebecca, are you coming to bed?"

"In a little while. I thought I would take some milk and cookies outside to eat. It's nice out now."

"You'll have a million bugs."

"I won't let any in the house."

Instead of milk I took a bucket of warm water, rags,

and a can of scouring powder with me through the back door. The smooth slates were easily cleaned, but the rough concrete clung to yellow chalk wraiths of the hateful words.

In the quiet night, *Red* and *Jew*, though now only in my head, seemed to be bellowing down the canyon of the facing houses and rolling on the asphalt of the street. Who are you there who hates us so, I thought. Is it that we're different? Because I have heavy dark hair that won't lie flat, instead of fine blond hair and pale skin with freckles? Or is it not the way I look, but what Papa says that you hate? That something must be wrong if so many people are out of work and hungry. If men are forced to leave their families and live in shantytowns made from packing boxes and hammered-down tin cans. Do you know, have you ever thought, how many empty cans of beans it takes to make a house? Even the smallest house? What it must be like to live between walls that are the garbage of a thousand unsatisfying meals cooked over a can of Sterno? To live chilled not only by the half-empty belly and the cold-collecting walls, but also by the realization that no one cares that you cling without hope to a world that doesn't want you?

A good man wants to come to Forgetown to say that we just can't let this happen and keep on happening. That men must be protected from a system that does this to them. But you say that he can't speak in your town. You make a sign on my house that says, I'm different, I'm bad. Now the tears, as real as my audience was fantasy, rolled over my cheeks. I sat on the bottom step, my chest heaving, trying to be quiet, wiping the tears with an end of one of the cleaning rags.

"Rebecca?" Mama called as I let myself into the house.

"Yes, Ma. I'm trying to decide if I want a cup of tea. How about you? Would you like some?"

"Tea? You just had milk. Me, I'm almost asleep."

I was in the kitchen, having just put away the cleaning things, when Papa came in. He looked strange. "Tell me, Rebecca, has anyone said anything to you? Anything mean or nasty, that your father is running for office as a Socialist?"

I thought of what I had wiped away an hour before. "Not said anything, no. Except Mr. Goldstein. He calls me 'the sheriff's daughter.' But that's just his idea of a joke. What made you think of that now?"

"Nothing. It just came into my mind. Are you going to bed? Tomorrow is a workday."

"In a minute. What about you?"

"I think maybe I'll make myself a glass of tea."

Papa's words sounded too much like mine to Mama. "Pa, I think you're trying to get me to go upstairs so you can do something outside. And I think I know what it is."

"What's to know?"

"Did someone write *Red* and *Jew* all over the sidewalk?"

"You went out? You saw?"

"I did more. I scrubbed it all up. Quietly, so Mama wouldn't know. Whoever did it must have watched me and then did it again. Up the front steps too?" Papa nodded. "That was the hardest to get off," I told him.

Papa thought for a minute. "Maybe I'll hook up the hose."

"I'll get the broom and sweep while you wash."

We had just finished cleaning the sidewalk when Samuel came home. Papa spoke up quickly. "Rebecca and I thought the lawn looked a little dry."

"So you decided to water it in the middle of the night? And if you're worrying about the lawn, why are you watering the sidewalk?"

I pointed to the risers. Samuel nodded. "Why don't you go to bed, Rebecca? I'll help Pa."

"It'll go faster if we all work," I said.

"I'd like to get my hands on whoever did this," Samuel said, sweeping a step angrily.

"Do you think it's a boy from the neighborhood?" I asked Papa.

He answered slowly. "I think it's a boy from someplace. I don't think a grown-up would do it. It's a child's trick."

"But where does a child learn ideas like that except from grown-ups?" I persisted.

"They learn from grown-ups—but the children do it. Grown-ups know you shouldn't write what you think in chalk. That's the only difference," Papa said.

Although we tried to be quiet, Mama heard us creeping up the stairs. I knew I would not be able to sleep unless I cooled off, so over Mama's objections about the hour, I filled the tub with cold water.

The porcelain was cool against my body; the water in which I was wrapped kept the heat at bay. But what, I wondered, would erase the pain of the words I had read?

If I used strong brown Octagon soap, as Mama did when she had suspected I had wandered into poison ivy, and the hottest water I could stand, I did not think I could scrub away the feeling that I had been branded. Deep down where they would not fade quickly were sharp bruises to my inner self, stubborn in their power to stay, like the yellow marks that clung to the concrete no matter how hard I tried to remove them.

Tomorrow I would go to work, would walk on Broadway and Easton Street, would have to look at Forgetown faces that hid such hatred of me, and of Papa, who only wanted things to be better. I wondered if it would ever be possible for men to listen to each other and to learn new ways to work together for everyone's good.

Samuel was up early and offered to walk me to work.

"All gone," he said as we stood on the sidewalk and searched for remnants of the marks we had erased in the dark.

"But if that's how people feel, what chance has Papa of finding a place for his meeting?" I asked.

"Not much, I guess."

After that we walked silently toward the store, where he left me, each of us carrying the memory of the yellow words.

The Papa who walked toward the Smart Set at six o'clock was a man with good news in his steps and the lilt of his body. I ran to meet him.

"The meeting. You found a place for the meeting."

"Maybe yes, maybe no. When everybody is together, if I have something to say, then I'll say it."

"You did. You did. I'm sure of it. Give me a hint."

"A hint. Hmmm." We had now started up the hill toward home. "Let me think." Papa was obviously stalling so that he would not give his secret away. "Remember what time of the year it is. That's your hint."

"What time of year? Before the election? Before school starts? What does the time of the year have to do with your finding a place for your meeting?"

"Ah," said Papa. "That's the puzzle you have to solve. Then you'll know where the meeting will be." He speeded up his step, whistling the "Toreador's Song" from *Carmen* to set a faster pace.

I could make no sensible connection between the time of the year and Papa's dilemma, but I knew he would tell me nothing more so I hurried after him, the sooner to get home to hear it all.

"Sophie, Samuel," he called as soon as he was inside the door. "I have news."

"You found a hall," Mama said.

"The Finnish church?" asked Samuel.

"Yes to Mama, no to Samuel," Papa told them. "I gave Rebecca a hint; it didn't help her, but you should have the same. Think what time of the year it is." More "Toreador's Song" as Mama and Samuel and I looked at each other and shrugged our shoulders.

"Time to get ready for fall." Papa stopped whistling to encourage us with another tidbit. "Time to consider the fall wardrobe." Six more bars of whistling. "All right, I see you'll never get it. It's the end of August, right? And always the end of August Celia Wallington comes for a suit. Though this year, to tell you the truth, with the

(60)

Works still closed, I wondered. To make a long story short, as soon as I opened after lunch, in she comes. Right away to the books to look for a style. But then maybe she notices I'm quiet, I'm worried. 'Mr. Levine,' she says, 'you have something on your mind.' So I tell her. 'Cluck, cluck,' she says and asks, 'how many people do you think will come?' 'Two hundred, maybe two fifty,' I say. All the time I'm figuring, now comes the lecture why do I waste my time associating with people who want to destroy the free enterprise system. But no, no. Instead she says—and I can hardly believe my ears—'If we open the doors between the front parlor and the library, we can set up two hundred folding chairs. It's ridiculous to think you'll have more. You'll be lucky to get a hundred. If you do, they can sit on the stairs—it's perfectly comfortable. I used to watch the dancing from there when I was a little girl.' So I say, 'You mean, we could use your house? You know a lot of people will come just out of curiosity.' She isn't bothered by that at all. 'You'll need anybody you can get, no matter what reason they come for,' she says. 'Don't be so sure,' I tell her. 'Almost a million people voted for Mr. Thomas in 1932, and times haven't gotten much better.' So she says, 'Not many of that million live in Wainford County, so I don't expect to be swamped.' And I can't help myself, I have to ask: 'Tell me, Mrs. Wallington, surely you don't approve of what Mr. Thomas says?' And she tells me, 'Frankly, my husband thinks he's terrible, but my mother went to school with his mother, and always said she was a lovely girl.' So I shake her hand and I tell her, 'On behalf of the entire executive committee of the Wainford

(61)

County Socialist Party, I want to say thank you, and I want you to know, should I become sheriff, I wouldn't forget what you did.' "

"Oh, Papa. Mrs. Wallington's. Nobody I know has ever been there." I pictured the white house, high on the slope of Broadway. As Mama and Samuel crowded closer to Papa, pressing for more details to extend the time of good news, I wondered if the entrance of the Levine family into Mrs. Wallington's house was the symbol of a different kind of life we might lead if Papa were really elected sheriff. Perhaps the sheriff's daughter could enter places that plain Rebecca Levine could not. Gates that always seemed to be closing as I approached would now open effortlessly. The half-glass partition that imprisoned me at my desk at the Smart Set would dissolve, and I would be invited to enter a world where people spoke, not of ledgers and inventories, but of books and ideas.

Chapter 7

As September neared I wondered what would now mark the seasons. Before this the rhythm of my days had been determined by the school calendar. My years had always begun with the opening of school. For me the celebration of Rosh Hashanah, the Jewish New Year, in September or early October—not the other in the middle of winter —seemed to be the time to make a fresh start. This year school would open on September second; the Jewish New Year would begin on the seventeenth.

For Samuel September second was no different from any other school morning in Forgetown. Heshie was on the front porch as we came out, in new slacks and a clean white shirt instead of the old clothes he had worn all summer. The outdoor work had tanned his face and arms and bleached his hair several shades lighter. "You look so grown-up, Rebecca," he said. It had taken me the whole summer at twenty-five cents a week to pay Mrs. Goldstein for my blouse. It was sailor-blue, piped at the collar, cuffs, and down the placket, which was on the left side, in light gray. Papa had made a matching pale gray skirt from wool he had found on sale on one of his trips into the city. It had sharp pleats marked with embroidered inverted V's of matching silk at the knees, where the skirt opened out to give me walking room.

I thanked Heshie, but could not help adding, "But I wish I were wearing it to the first day of school, instead of to the Smart Set."

"And I wish I was going anyplace except school," he answered as we started down the hill. "All those old maids telling you, 'Do this, do that,' all day long."

We separated at the intersection of Broadway and Easton Street, where I walked left on Easton to work, and they went right to Cross Street and school. I looked back after half a block and saw that Heshie was watching me. I waved and turned again toward the Smart Set, thinking that we each envied the way the other was spending September second.

All about me students were talking and laughing on their way to Cross Street. I wanted to get into the store quickly so that I could march smartly to my desk, throw open the big ledger, and survey my neat rows of figures. Then I could recover at least a sense of order and importance. Instead I had to stand outside, looking anxiously for Mr. Goldstein's tan Chevrolet.

At ten minutes of nine Mr. and Mrs. Goldstein arrived. Each issued a brief good-morning. Longer opening phrases were reserved for mornings when something was wrong. This, then, was the way the new year began, with no distinction from the old. I opened the ledger to enter the morning's invoices.

At dinner I questioned Samuel about my favorite teachers and the few friends who were still in school. He was not nearly so eager to answer as I had been to ask. Instead, he talked to Papa about the election. Thereafter, every time I tried to talk to Samuel about school, he talked about something else.

On the second day of Rosh Hashanah we found out why. We were waiting for Mama in the downstairs hall when a car with an insignia we could see but not decipher stopped at our door. The man who got out of the car did not look familiar. We had all stepped out on the porch, including Mama, who had just finished adjusting the veil on her good black velvet hat, as he came up the walk. It was uncommonly warm, and we were all uncomfortable in the winter clothes we traditionally started wearing at this, the beginning of another year.

"Meyer Levine?" he asked Papa, who nodded in reply. "I'm Charles Howard, the truant officer." He turned to Samuel. "And this must be the missing Samuel—"

"What do you mean, missing? He isn't missing," Mama interrupted, unwilling to admit what she must have known he meant.

"From school, Ma," Samuel answered. "He means I haven't been in school all year."

"How could that be? Every day I made your lunch, and every day you left for school on time."

"Just because he left for school doesn't mean that he arrived at school. That's what they call playing hooky," Papa explained dryly.

"I think I should sit down," Mama said. We all moved away so that she could get to the glider. After she sat down at one end, I sat at the other. Samuel and the two men turned to face us.

"I'm sorry to have to upset you about this, Mrs. Levine," Mr. Howard said. "But after a long unexplained absence state law requires that we go to the home to speak to the parents. I could come another time. You seem to be on your way someplace."

"To the synagogue," Papa explained. "It's the second day of the holiday celebrating the beginning of a new year. This is a way for a year to begin?" He addressed the last to Samuel, who looked as though he was getting still warmer in his best wool suit.

"I could come back Monday, since this is your holiday," Mr. Howard offered.

"No, I couldn't go to the synagogue with this on my mind anyway. Let's hear the worst."

"The first week of school your son came to classes for two days. Since then, not at all. It's been almost two weeks. Of course he's sixteen and we can't make him go to school anymore. But it is school-board policy to make an effort to get every child who enters the high school to stay until he graduates. These days you have to have a high school diploma if you want to get anywhere."

"That's what I tell him all the time. Without an education you're nothing. But do you think he listens?"

Samuel finally spoke out. "Mama, you always think school and books is the only way to learn anything. But you won't see that school and I don't get along."

Mama was prepared to answer with a tirade, but Papa stopped her by asking Samuel mildly, "So if not school, what then? Do you expect to work? And if so, at what?"

"I planned to tell you tonight. After *shul*. Heshie and I want to work at our lawn-cutting business."

"Would that be Hershel Greenspan?" asked Mr. Howard. When Samuel agreed, he added, "I have to see his parents next. I suppose they'll be in the synagogue too."

We all nodded in unison.

But Mama was not to be distracted from Samuel's announcement. "How can you cut lawns in winter?"

"In winter we'll shovel snow." Samuel sounded less certain now, as though remembering the cold on the streets of Forgetown when the wind came from the west off the river.

Papa spoke up. "I see that we all have a lot to talk about. Meanwhile, I think, now we should go to *shul*. The talking will wait until later. Mr. Howard, you did your job. You told us our son was a truant. Now we have to see if we can talk him and his friend into staying in school."

I had not yet really taken in this fresh blow to my hopes for college. Samuel was moving farther away from the day when he might be able to help support Mama and Papa. Instead, his leaving school added another link to the chain that would bind me to the Smart Set until I was too old to do anything else. We walked to *shul* then.

The normally solemn occasion was made more so by the uncomfortable knowledge we had never before faced a crisis like this. One of us had deceived the others, had pretended something was so that was not. Mama and Papa must have felt as cheated as I did. Each morning I had envied Samuel as he marched off. I imagined the welcome meetings with his friends, the calling and laughing down the halls, the teacher's admiration of a good term paper or a well-written test. School was a place where I had been somebody. Not so the Smart Set. There I was the one who was blamed for goods that were misplaced or errands not done. It even seemed in some mysterious way to be my fault if not enough customers came into the shop, or if those who came did not buy.

Yet Samuel, who could have still enjoyed what was denied me, played truant instead. Mama's harangue to Samuel started as soon as we closed the door on the ringing "good *yontifs*" of the Toplinskys, who had walked home from *shul* with us, before going on up the hill to their own holiday dinner. "All day in *shul* did I *daven*? No, I bit my lips and held my hands to keep from shaking you to find out how you could do such a thing. *How* could you do such a thing? How could you pretend you went to school every day and instead you went God-knows-where with your friend? How?"

"Sophie, even if the boy had an answer, who could hear? Take off your hat and coat, and Rebecca will help you get dinner. Then we'll talk."

As Mama clicked the soup tureen down on the dining room table, I could see that not only the food, but her anger at Samuel had heated as she stood over the stove.

"Weeks I planned and saved and did without so we should have a nice dinner on the holiday, and now to eat it's like straw."

"It smells delicious, Sophie. Maybe if we all try for a few minutes to forget what's on our minds, we can still enjoy it a little."

In silence Mama started to eat while I tried to make everyone think of something else. "Papa," I asked, deciding on the subject only after he looked up. "Do you think you'll be able to get enough people to come to Mrs. Wallington's so that it won't be embarrassing?"

Papa looked grateful for the chance to talk about something other than Samuel's delinquency. "Maybe you and Samuel could make a few signs about it, and I could ask in the stores to put them up."

"Heshie and I thought we could go to New Vernon too, and put signs in a few windows. Maybe somebody there would like to hear Mr. Thomas."

"Why not?" Papa agreed. "Maybe tomorrow, when there's no school." The first mention of Mr. Thomas's speech had so obscured Samuel's truancy that Papa forgot that the opening and closing of school was of scant importance to his son.

Mama, however, had not. "What's the difference to him, school or no school?"

"All right, Sophie, we said no discussion while we eat."

After that we ate in silence. Mama's chicken soup with homemade noodles, the golden roast bird, the steaming potatoes, the sweet-and-sour cabbage, fell on stomachs ready to turn them to bile. When he had taken the cup of tea offered by Mama, Papa stood up. "'Tea I can drink in the living room. Now that the condemned man has had a hearty meal, we can see about his execution."

Samuel and I could not help smiling at Papa's words, but Mama glared at Papa's back as she followed him into the living room, the cup of her good dinner set—sweetheart roses on eggshell pottery—shaking against the saucer. Papa sat at one end of the sofa, she at the other, Samuel and I on the chairs in opposing corners.

Mama spoke first. "So now it's time? Now I can ask my son what he has to do that is more important than getting an education he should be somebody?"

"What has learning 'Two points determine a line' got to do with being anybody? School is just a place I have to be until you say I can stop going. Only this year it's so bad, we just decided not to go at all. Mr. Howard said the law says we don't have to go to school if we're sixteen. Only the board of education would like us to. That's because the state pays them to teach us, that's why."

"But without a high school diploma what can you make from your life?" Mama persisted.

"My life will be what it is because of me, not because of some piece of paper. Look at all the men with high school diplomas, or like Cousin Jacob, with college degrees even, who can't get work. The only ones who are helped by my education are the teachers who get paid to tell me things I don't need to know. Except to get good marks on the tests they make up to show how good they are at teaching."

Papa spoke before Mama had a chance to. "What he

says has some truth," Papa says. "Plenty of educated men are without work."

Mama pivoted on her end of the sofa to face him. "So that means that you are happy that your son is going to leave school and be a bum."

"No. It only means that I am agreeing with one of the things he said. Just because I agree with one thing doesn't mean I am happy with what he wants to do." Papa looked straight at Samuel, "You know we want very much you should finish school. It's only this year and next. You see how upset Mama is. Are you sure what you are doing is right? Maybe you should finish high school, just in case you ever need it."

Samuel started to cry then. His face was still tan from the summer. It glistened now with the tears he wiped away with the back of his hand, only as they reached his chin.

"But to lie to us. Since the beginning of school. To lie." Mama was crying now too, dabbing at her eyes with the handkerchief she usually wore tucked in her cuff.

"I knew it wouldn't be good, whenever I told you."

"All right, so now we know. What will be now?" Papa asked.

"I told you. Heshie and I thought we would try to keep our business going."

"Business. You call that a business?" Mama removed the handkerchief to look at her son.

"Why not? We do a job, we get paid."

"But it's only a job. It's no kind of business for a

Jewish boy. And if there's no grass to cut, you maybe stop eating?"

"Look, look, we'll get no place this way," Papa said, stopping Mama. "Samuel, tell me. Would it be possible, you and Heshie to go to school and still run your business? Maybe instead of geometry you should study bookkeeping, like Rebecca, and learn something you could use."

"But bookkeeping. How can we study bookkeeping? That's for girls."

I was happy to be able to say something at last. "No," I told them. "Not just for girls. In my class there were five boys."

"Today we are all upset. But Monday I could go to see the principal and tell him you don't think you will use what you are learning. I'll ask him to let you change, and you'll try for a while. That's right, you'll try for a while?"

"For a while. To the Christmas holidays anyway."

"That's not long enough to tell, but let it be like that for now. Later we'll talk about it some more. Is that all right, Sophie?" Mama's face was completely covered by her handkerchief, and she nodded without answering.

"What will I tell Heshie? We planned this together."

"You call him now to come over here. I'll tell him what I told you. We'll see if I can convince him too."

When Heshie came, he sat silently on the piano stool while Papa repeated his arguments. At the end, when Samuel nodded to show that he had been convinced, Heshie nodded as well and said he would tell his parents that he had decided to go back to school.

Each time Heshie spoke, he looked to Samuel. I knew

he was agreeing to go back to school just because Samuel wished it, and that Samuel was doing it because our parents wanted it so. Each perfunctory nod seemed to chip away at my chances of changing my life. I believed with Mama that without his diploma Samuel would never make anything of himself and as Mama was, I was consoled, however temporarily, that he had agreed to return to school.

Before Heshie left for home, he stopped me in the hall. "Is this what you want too, Rebecca? I don't mind going back to school so much if I know you want me to."

"It's not easy to tell other people what to do. But I think Mama and Papa are right about needing an education to be somebody. To do something important with your life."

He shook his head. "You make it sound so easy. If I finish school, I'll be someone. If I don't, I won't. I'm not so sure. But if it's what you want. . . ."

"I think it's what you both should be doing now," I said slowly, wondering if I was suggesting not what was best for Heshie and Samuel, but best for me and my need to get out of the Smart Set.

September twenty-ninth was a bright, mild day that crisped into evening. After supper we left the house together: Mama in her best suit and black velvet hat that she always wore to *shul*; Papa in his gray herringbone jacket, now reunited with the trousers, and a new tie of figured maroon silk; Samuel in his good navy blue suit; me in my new fall blouse and skirt. We walked past Papa's shop, the Smart Set, the other shops darkened for the night, and up the hill. The Wallingtons' house seemed to have a light on in every room. Three stories high with a wraparound porch, it stood white and splendid on the top of Broadway. Although it was early, a line of cars already filled one side of the street.

"A lot of people," Papa said with satisfaction.

Mrs. Wallington met us at the door, where Papa made the necessary introductions. She was wearing her new gabardine suit and looked, I thought, like a woman who belonged in that house. She and Papa walked away talking busily, while we went on by ourselves.

The walls of the hallway were paneled white halfway up, with blue and white wallpaper above and darkly glowing floors below. In the first room we entered, we saw a cream-colored marble fireplace and wallpaper with red velvet flowers. All the furniture had been removed from that room, as well as the one beyond, which was lined with bookcases painted white like the hall paneling. Rows of wooden chairs from the undertakers had been set out in both rooms. As we moved into the library to be nearer the speakers, we saw that there were already more than two dozen people assembled. Up front Mrs. Wallington and Papa seemed to be discussing the arrangement of the chairs and lectern. Mama and Samuel and I spoke to the people we knew on our way to find seats.

"That Mrs. Cantor from the candy store," Mama whispered to me, "she's no more a Socialist than the man in the moon. Just nosy."

"Didn't the suit look good on Mrs. Wallington?" I said. "And did you see the pin she has on the lapel? I never saw rhinestones sparkle so."

"That's because they're diamonds," Mama said. "That's why they sparkle."

With relief I saw that people were beginning to come in faster now, everyone dressed in his best and treating the evening as an important event. All of them, except old Mrs. Morris, who never seemed to notice where she was, were exceedingly interested in the details of the room. I saw Mrs. Feldman touching the flowers on the wallpaper to make sure they really were velvet and not just printed to look that way.

At eight thirty silence spread from the back of the parlor through the archway to the hall as we saw a tall man being led by Marty Grogan to the front. There he shook hands with Papa and Ed Feldman before sitting down in the center chair. The hum of talk resumed. Papa stood up, one arm raised, until the audience was quiet.

"Ladies and gentlemen, Mrs. Wallington, who was kind enough to let us use her house, and Mr. Thomas, who honors us with his presence . . . good evening," he said.

I had not told anyone that twice during the past month on my way back to the Smart Set after lunch, I had seen Papa practicing his speech in front of the pier glass, arms flung back, feet apart, head thrust forward. I had feared he would look foolish in front of all these people. Instead, he spoke easily, as though speech-making was as natural for him as tailoring, the familiar singsong tamed by the pauses he injected for dramatic effect. He ended by mentioning his son, Samuel, and Samuel's question about the job of a sheriff.

"I had to tell him about what sheriffs *really* do these

days, and when I did, I thought something is wrong if an elected official's job is to move poor people from their homes instead of protecting their rights to stay there. And so it is especially important, when times are so bad for the working man, that we have someone like Norman Thomas to lead us to find better ways. And we here in Forgetown are fortunate that he was able to come to this out-of-the-way place to speak to us. . . . Mr. Norman Thomas."

The tallest man I had ever seen unwrapped his long legs and stood up from the center chair. I was not surprised to see that Mr. Thomas was taller than Papa, who was not big, but he also towered over Marty Grogan, who stood at six feet. Mr. Thomas spoke for a long time without once looking at a note or seeming to strain for a word. The audience listened carefully, and although I knew that I was hearing a great man, I let his words flow around me without stopping as I floated free from worry, now that Papa's part of the program was past. The evening ended in a blur of applause, smiles, and good-byes ringing in the September night. Our return home was quickened both by the terrain, downhill all the way, and our pride in Papa's performance as a politician.

Two days after the meeting Mama had a peculiar request for Papa. "Do you have some pamphlets or books I could read about Socialism?"

"What do you think the children have been mailing out all summer?"

"Those, yes. But something more complete. With answers to questions people might ask."

"How come all of a sudden, five weeks before the election, you want to know so much about Socialism?"

"I have to speak at a meeting."

Papa, Samuel, and I all spoke together.

"*Nu*, another politician."

"Are you sure you know how to make a speech?"

"Can we come and hear you?"

"Tuesday night, at Mrs. Wallington's," Mama said, "Mrs. Cantor asked me would I come a week from Wednesday to her reading group. Instead of literature they are going to have politics. She asked would I talk about Socialism. A five-minute speech. I said yes."

"What will you tell them, Ma?" Samuel asked.

"What I remember from Mr. Thomas's speech. I came home and I wrote down what was important so I wouldn't forget. And then I thought I would read a little, so in case they ask me questions, I'll have answers."

"I'll go to the library lunchtime and see what they have that you can read in a week," I said.

I explained to the librarian that the books I wanted were for my mother, who was about to launch herself on a public-speaking career.

"I hadn't realized, Rebecca, that it was *your* father who was running on the Socialist ticket. Has he always been a Socialist?"

"As long as I can remember. He always said we have to try to find new ways to help people because the old ways aren't working. And we're all helping in the campaign."

"You have to help your own father. . . . But you always seemed so quiet, how can you believe in violence and revolution?"

"I don't. It's the Communists who believe that you have to have a revolution to give the proletariat control. They even have their own candidate, Earl Browder. But we believe in peaceful change. Norman Thomas has been a pacifist most of his life. That's what my mother wants to talk about, explaining the difference."

"Well, these should help her." She checked out the books we had selected together and pushed the pile across the counter to me.

After dinner Mama settled herself at the dining room table, where for so many years I had done my homework each night. I had never before seen Mama doing work that did not deal with the physical comfort of her family. She laboriously covered three-by-five cards with small seldom used script. I feared that she was preparing to tell her listeners far more than they were willing to hear. However, I couldn't think of a tactful way to suggest she might bore her audience. Samuel, less mindful of tact, could be more direct.

"Ma, they're just going to walk out on you if you give them all the stuff you have on those cards."

"But everything I have to tell them is important."

"People have been trying to tell me things they thought were important since the first grade, and I know how easy it is to sit still and pretend you're listening. After about three minutes of that"—Samuel indicated the cards with his head—"you'll be talking to the walls."

"But these women want to learn. Otherwise why would they come?"

"I don't know. But if you were told five minutes, you should talk for five."

"He's right, Ma," I agreed. "But not because it's you. With any speaker it would be the same."

At night, while Mama made notes, I worked on my secret file. At my desk during the day I jotted down bits of overheard conversations, or vignettes of arrivals and departures. In the evenings I added the details I remembered and entered them in my old loose-leaf notebook so that I would have material for letters to Max. Each of my days was a carbon copy of the first day I had spent at the Smart Set, so if I were to amuse or interest Max at all, it would have to be by imagining stories from these bits and pieces of other lives.

When a letter came from Max, I would go through my notebook and over several evenings work out an answer. Even though I took extra time to polish and revise, I noticed his replies were always slower than mine and seldom as long.

Three nights before Mama was to speak, her "homework" ended. She marched into the dining room after answering the phone and slammed the books closed. Then she carefully shredded the cards. I watched her from the hallway.

"What's wrong, Ma?"

"When people are born ignorant, they die ignorant."

"Who's ignorant?" I knew she would have to tell me in her own way.

"That Rose Cantor. With her 'reading group' and her 'literary ladies.' " Mama's words were heaped with scorn that rolled over them like her rich brown gravy over the boiled potatoes she served. "They try to act smart and only show how ignorant they are. She tells me that they call her up and say that if I talk about Socialism, they won't come to her meeting. And she listens. It's useless to talk to them anyway. *Shkotzim* like Father Coughlin or Gerald Smith they'll listen to, but a chance to learn something—never."

"Oh, Mama. After all your work."

"Never mind the work. *I* learned. But they'll never learn. And Papa thinks they will vote for him. He should know they don't even want to be in the same room with a Socialist."

"Maybe if Papa talked to Mrs. Cantor tomorrow and told her how much work you did—"

"Too late now. I tore up the notes. Besides, on bended knees they could come to me now and I wouldn't speak."

But Wednesday, when the meeting was held, Mama turned the radio up loud. She took a long time over the dinner dishes. Saying she was tired, she went to bed early. Papa looked sad when he watched her. But his determination to speak to as many people as he could never wavered. That evening, as on the ones before and after, he left in his old car for the far corners of the county.

Chapter 8

The last Tuesday in October Mama, Papa, and I were at breakfast when Samuel, instead of dashing in at the last possible moment, came downstairs just as we were starting to eat. We gasped in unison as he entered the kitchen. His lip was puffed and cut. His right eye was darkened and swollen nearly closed. Coming in late from Heshie's the night before, he had been able to get to his room without being seen. Now Mama didn't give him a chance to talk. "What happened? You had an accident? In the car?"

"No accident, Ma. It's not serious. I purposely came down early so you could see it was nothing."

"If not an accident, so what happened?" Papa asked.

"Some dumb kids started a fight on the corner near the

Greenspans, and when Heshie and I went out to break it up, they hit us too. I know it looks terrible. But honest, it doesn't hurt. I'll get kidded plenty though."

"Right after breakfast, Meyer, you should go with him to the doctor," Mama decided.

"Don't worry, Ma. I don't need a doctor for a fat lip and a black eye. Rebecca, I'll walk with you as far as the store."

"You're sure you don't need a doctor?" Mama did not let go of an idea easily.

"I'm sure it's nothing that won't be better in a week. Come on, Rebecca."

"I don't want to sound like Mama, but maybe you should see a doctor." I paused at the bottom of the steps and turned Samuel so I could see his face in daylight.

"It's all right," he said, spinning away so that I saw less than I wanted to, shaking his head as if to throw off my glance. "But it didn't happen the way I said. They were waiting for me when I left here after supper. I thought Papa and Mama would worry if I told them the truth. Two of them. The big one started hitting me and saying, 'You Commie Jew bastard, why don't you go back where you came from?' They were just kids, but tough. The littler one tried to get me too, but I could take care of him. Then they knocked me down and, while I was getting up, ran like hell. I knew Papa would feel terrible if he thought his running for sheriff did this. I sneaked into Heshie's and he helped me clean up. But I wanted you to know, so that you'll be careful. After the election this'll stop. Meanwhile Heshie and I will come and walk you home from work."

"Two of them. Two against one. That's not fair. You should go to the police. They'll do something."

"What could they do? Make my eye heal faster? In a week the election will be over. Then everyone will forget. For now, better leave it alone, and be a little careful."

"That's awful. And they didn't even know the difference between a Socialist and a Communist. That's really dumb."

"If they knew, so they'd just say 'Socialist Jew bastard' instead of 'Commie Jew bastard.' They'd hit just as hard."

"Of course. I'm the dumb one. Listen, are you sure you feel okay? You don't want me to go with you to the doctor? I could tell Mr. Goldstein I'll be a little late."

Samuel shook his head. "I don't need a doctor. If I did, I would go."

"Didn't you recognize them? It's not such a big town that two tough kids could beat you up and you wouldn't know one of them."

Samuel didn't answer, and when I stopped walking to study him for the reason, he speeded up and motioned for me to do the same. "It doesn't matter if I think I know who it was. I'm not going to do anything about it until after the election."

"That means you know. Why won't you say?"

"Because I'm going to take care of it myself. And you'd better get inside. Mrs. Goldstein looks ready to pop her buttons."

I hurried inside where, as Samuel said, Mrs. Goldstein waited impatiently by the door. Mrs. Carter, who always behaved as if fearful that she might do something to anger her employer, stood at attention at her post in the back, next to the stacked-up boxes of hosiery. She nodded and said good morning to me without once turning her eyes from Mrs. Goldstein.

The memory of *Red* and *Jew* all over our sidewalk, my brother's torn lip and damaged eye, were hurts that must be avenged. I wanted to tell the police, the newspaper, people on the street. I could not even be sure that the danger had ended. Perhaps as Papa drove about the dark streets of Forgetown in his De Soto, bullies waited to harm him as well.

Election Day was a week away. School would be closed, and the shopkeepers expected to be busy. If I wanted to have the day off, I had to arrange it now. Feeling the pain of Samuel's bruises as though they were my own, I knew I could not sit out Election Day at my desk. I beckoned to Mr. Goldstein through the glass, and trying to sound casual, made my request as he walked in.

"Oh, so the sheriff's daughter wants to get into politics too. Doesn't any of the Levines think it might be a good idea just to do a job and let someone else worry about society?"

"But I'm never sick. I haven't missed one day's work since I started here," I answered, sidestepping the argument. "But this is important. I don't think it's asking too much to have the day off. I don't expect to get paid."

"Of course not. Who would pay if you don't work? So take the day off if it's so important. But you'll have to do more on Wednesday to make up for what you miss."

"I expect to."

He left my office then. I spent the day channeling my wish for revenge into neat columns and rows of well-formed digits. As Samuel had promised he and Heshie were waiting for me at six o'clock, when Mr. Goldstein closed the store. I was glad it was dark, for the sight of Samuel's bruises made my own face hurt.

Before we left Broadway, I heard my name called and saw Janet running toward me from the five-and-ten, where she had been a cashier for two months. She earned even less than I did at the Smart Set and hated her job as much as I did mine. Since school had ended, we no longer had much in our dull lives to discuss with each other. The fantasies that had sustained us had evaporated.

The best of our classmates had left Forgetown. Fred Hickens was at Northwestern on a scholarship. Joe Solomon and his family had moved to Detroit, where Mr. Solomon's brother had a job for him. Marcia Feldman was at State College. Janet and I were stranded, guiltily avoiding the knowledge that we could not help each other. I knew that she must have something special to tell me if she had waited here to intercept me.

"It's about the election, Rebecca," she said as we dropped behind the boys. "I had to explain to you that my father won't be voting. I wanted you to know. He said he would have liked to vote for your father because he always thought you came from a very nice family. But he didn't go out to register. You know why. So he can't vote."

"I never thought your father would consider voting for a Socialist."

(85)

"That's why I had to tell you. He said he never liked Jim Tucker, and it would have been a great pleasure to have voted him out of office."

"Thank you for telling me. It's good to know that someone would vote for Papa if he could."

"I wish we were old enough to vote. I think maybe a few Socialists in Washington might help. Look at my daddy. Because he can't get a job, he won't vote."

"I wonder how many more men in Forgetown there are like your father."

"Not many who would hide for a year because they won't admit they don't have a job."

"Maybe more than we know. I sometimes think a lot of people must just be hiding out from the Depression."

"You know, don't you, that I want your father to win?"

"I hope so." I hugged Janet. "I thought everyone was against him. But I guess he has a few friends."

It would be easier to walk around Forgetown and look at the faces of people who came into the Smart Set or passed me on Easton Street if I could remember that not all of them thought, as Mr. Goldstein did, that Papa was foolish, or as the boys who wrote on our steps did, that he was wicked. Some people knew he was a good man, even though it seemed like the big, noisy ones were our enemies and the quiet, hidden ones our friends.

"Pa, Heshie and I want to go with you for the rest of the campaign," Samuel said at dinner.

"What's the matter? No homework?"

"Maybe it's more important to see a candidate at work than to read about elections in some dumb book."

"There you have a point. Come with me if you want."

I knew that Mama was biting back her objections, so I quickly chimed in with my approval. I was relieved that Papa would have two young bodyguards.

On Friday I was surprised to see only Heshie waiting outside the Smart Set. "Where's Samuel?" I asked.

"He's busy, and he asked me to come for you."

"What's he busy with now?"

Silence. Heshie was poor at thinking up stories to cover up Samuel's secrets.

"He's not in trouble in school, is he?"

Heshie shook his head.

"It's about the election. Did he get hurt again?" The thought came late, but when it did, the picture of Samuel hurt and alone twisted my voice.

Heshie was forced to calm me. "No, no, it's not that."

"How can I be sure if you don't tell me what it is?"

He thought over my question and sighed. "You win. He heard some boys talking in school. They're going out to the cemetery tonight and knock over the stones."

I pictured Abraham's small headstone in the middle row. "Tonight?"

"Mischief Night. The night before Halloween."

"But where's Samuel now?"

"He's rounding up as many Jewish kids as he can get. He wants to be there when they come."

"I'm coming too."

"But you're a girl."

"It's my brother who's buried there. I have a right to help protect his grave."

"Samuel won't like it."

(87)

"I'll take care of Samuel," I added. "What are you going to do when you get there?"

"I don't think we thought about that."

I had begun to, but said nothing to Heshie. After dinner I motioned Samuel out to the porch.

I spoke quickly. "I know all about it and I've been thinking. When they get to the cemetery, we should come from behind the headstones dressed in sheets and making the scariest noises we can."

As I spoke I could see Samuel's expression turn from dismay at my discovery to admiration for the suggestion. "Good idea."

"And I'm going to be there. And I'd like to bring Janet too. She wants to help. She told me so."

"No girls."

"If you don't let us come, I'll tell Papa right now."

Both of us knew I wasn't bluffing. My chances of going would not diminish if Papa were in charge.

"All right. But just two. Don't go finding any more friends. Eight promised to come besides Heshie and us. That's plenty."

"I don't have any more friends. How will you tell them about the sheets?"

"I'll call a couple and tell them to pass the word."

"And I'll walk over and get Janet. Should we all meet in front of the school? No one hangs around there at night, and it's not too far to the cemetery."

I carried my coat upstairs to my room. There I removed the top sheet from my bed, replacing the bedspread carefully. I folded the sheet lengthwise in quarters, lifted my sweater, and wrapped the sheet cocoonlike about my body. Two large safety pins at my breast and waist held it in place. I pulled my sweater over the top and concealed everything with my coat.

Two of Samuel's friends, both carrying oddly shaped bundles were already in front of the school when Janet and I arrived.

The four of us stood uncomfortably avoiding each other's eyes like early guests at a party. As I was beginning to worry that the others had met elsewhere and gone on without us, we heard footsteps and saw Samuel, Heshie, and six other boys turn the corner from Broadway.

When Samuel saw us, he conducted his group into a U-turn with a flourish. We ran to catch up with the line, hurrying back toward Broadway and down the hill to the river. Samuel nodded to Heshie, who dropped back until he reached Janet and me.

I suspected he had been assigned to guard us, but instead of mentioning it, I admired the way he had stuffed his sheet under his jacket.

"I thought at first I'd never get it buttoned. It makes me feel like a sausage," he said. "I'll be glad to get rid of it." And then he added, "I wonder how many of them will come?"

I had been carried along by excitement and thoughts of revenge, certain that these would be the boys who had written on the walk and beaten Samuel. I had not thought that some of us might get hurt. "Do you think that there might be more of them than there are of us?"

"Good chance," Heshie answered. "Making mischief in a cemetery should be a popular stunt."

Janet looked as though she, too, realized for the first time that there might be violence. "We can drop you by the Sweet Shop if you want to change your mind," I told her. "It's always bright there, and we can pick you up on the way back."

She shook her head. "If you can go, I can go."

After that we speeded up to catch up with the others, whom Samuel was urging into a trot. I thought of something I had forgotten for years. Once, before Samuel was old enough to go to school, he had come in crying from a morning in front of the house with the boys on the street. When Mama asked why, she was told that the other children had said that the Jews were bad because they killed the Lord. Mama comforted him with cookies. Papa had other sentiments. When Samuel repeated his story for Papa, he thought a long time.

"What can you tell a four-year-old child?" he asked Mama categorically. "But something—you have to explain," he answered himself. "Samuel," he said, "people who say that want an excuse to hate Jews. If you want to, you can tell them the Romans killed Jesus. That is true. Better you should tell them to read what Jesus tried to teach. To love others, not to value property more than people. That's enough for a start. If they'll listen."

We waited to hear what would happen the next time Samuel played with those children. "Well," Papa asked him, "did you tell them what I told you about Jesus?"

"No."

"You mean you said nothing?" Mama asked.

"Oh, no. I told them if they catch *our* Lord, they can kill Him."

We laughed then at the table, in great wrenching gulps, our faces red and glistening with tears. I thought now as I ran behind Samuel's followers that he had taken up the challenge again. I wanted to tell Janet the story I had remembered but I needed all my breath for running.

In the last quarter of a mile Samuel slackened the pace. I was sure that he did not think it would be respectful for us to enter the cemetery panting and disheveled. I did what I could to make myself look neater.

We stopped just inside the stone walls. Samuel drew us into a circle. "It looks like we beat them. Now, here's what we'll do. Take out your sheets." A general rustle of clothes and fabric. I turned away from the others to unpin my sheet and pull it out from under my sweater and coat.

"Put it on like a cape. But keep an end to throw over your head later." More rustling. "Everybody get behind a stone. Crouch down. Don't peek out. Heshie will be on the hill under the tree, watching the road. If he hears something, he'll tell Seymour on the end, and we'll pass it on. Make sure you don't leave spaces between. Otherwise you won't get the word and won't be ready."

We broke the circle to grope our way whitely among the pale gray stones. I hurried to Abraham's grave and motioned Janet to its neighbor, which belonged to Harriet Greenspan's mother. I felt at home in my usual spot behind the headstone, but I thought Janet might be frightened in the darkness. "It's all right," I whispered. "She was a very nice lady." I pointed to the headstone. "Heshie's grandma. She used to make *rugalach* and give them to us kids when we went there to visit. They're

yummy pastries with lots of butter and raisins and nuts."
It helped to think about something good to eat instead of
where we were or what might happen.

Samuel crouched behind us. "Everyone's ready. Janet
will get the word from Jackie. He'll just say 'okay.' When
you hear him, Janet, you say 'okay' to Rebecca. Quietly.
After you tell Rebecca, you start counting to thirty. Rebecca, you say 'okay' to Morton and you count to twenty-
five. Got that? When you get to the last number you're
supposed to count to, jump up and make the most awful
noise you can and start toward the gate. Try to sort of
float, and, you know, flap your arms like a ghost. Good
luck."

Samuel went off to crouch behind the next two. Janet
and I went over our instructions to make sure we understood, and settled back. We moved only if we had to,
taking care to stay hidden behind the stones. It was like
being imprisoned in a small box. My arms and legs fell
asleep and my neck hardened into an aching column.
The cold seeped from the soles of my feet through my
tightly clenched thighs. When I could bear it no longer, I
would drop to my knees and straighten my back for a
few moments until the chill through my stockings forced
me to return to a crouch.

As the waiting grew painful I regretted that I had insisted on coming along. I knew I would spoil everything
if I stood up, but I didn't know if I could crouch any
longer.

Abruptly I sensed a change. The wind still rustled the
leaves, the branch of the old oak creaked, but I thought I

heard voices on the road. Then Janet whispered "okay"
—hoarsely and much too loud, it seemed. For a moment
I forgot what I was supposed to do. Morton, I remembered. I leaned to my left, making sure I kept the sheet
behind the headstone. "Okay." Back in my crouch I
started counting. ". . . twenty-one, twenty-two, twenty-
three, twenty-four, twenty-five. *Who-ooo-ooo.*" I stood
up slowly, trying to wail the sound. Blinded by the sheet
over my face but reassured by the wailing and rushing all
around, I headed toward the place where I thought the
gate was. I could only see a circle of blackness around
my feet while ruts, mounds, headstones, lurked all about
to throw me to the ground. Gradually the hooting and
calling that had been all about me died, and I lifted my
sheet to look. Including myself, eleven white figures were
scattered among the rows of stones.

"They're gone," said Samuel, the leader. We walked
toward his voice, uncoiling our sheets. Heshie ran down
the hill toward us.

"It was great. Absolutely great. I never saw anything
like it in my life. They had just started coming through
the gate, looking around, kind of. Then you all stood
up at the same time. And the noise." He laughed, remembering. "Even I was scared. And then, when you all
started toward them with your arms going, they just
turned and ran like hell. I counted six of them. They
must be on the other side of town by now."

"Did you recognize anyone?" I asked.

"Listen, it's dark. I was lucky I could see it was people."

We sang and laughed as we trooped through town, delivering the victorious foot soldiers to their barracks. Finally we had evened the score. We had made them turn and run. Now I had two bright spots to remember in the dark of Forgetown winter-to-come: Mischief Night and Max's kiss.

Election day was clear and cool. Samuel and I were both down to breakfast early, but Papa was already gone.

"To be there when the polls opened," Mama explained. "He wants to see who votes first, and how they look."

The telephone rang while we were still at the table. Ed Feldman gave us a list of people he thought might be too old or ill to go to the polls alone. Samuel and I were to walk with them to voting places or to find rides for them if necessary.

The first name on our list was that of Elvira Morris. She was over eighty and lived alone in the gabled gatehouse of what had been the biggest estate in Forgetown. As a child I had always thought that her house looked like the gingerbread house in *Hansel and Gretel*. Once or twice when Papa had taken me there, we sat together on the thin cushions of a polished walnut sofa. While Mrs. Morris and Papa talked, I tried to follow the faded designs on the small rugs dotting the floor. Just after Papa had been asked to run, we visited again. The bit of brightness from the blue-glass bottle collection was gone. The winter had been cold, and I suspected her bottles had been sold to pay the coal bill. We never would have learned of any financial difficulties from Mrs. Morris, herself, however. Her talk might be of the latest book of social change she had read, or some conclusion she had reached about the economy.

Papa told me that she did not have many visitors. But neither Mrs. Morris nor her house seemed neglected. I felt that the books she read kept the gingerbread house full of ideas, and that they were her company.

Mrs. Morris was so long in answering the bell that I was about to suggest to Samuel that we climb in a window to make sure she was all right. Just then she opened the door, smiling with welcome, shaking with age.

"Ah, Meyer's children. Come in, come in."

"We thought you might want some help getting to the polls," I told her. "We can even get someone to drive you."

"Oh, no, I'd rather walk. It's such a lovely day. And such nice young company." As Samuel helped her into the coat she plucked from a brass coat tree in the corner, she added, "You'd be surprised, it never bothered me before, but people think this house looks like the house in *Hansel and Gretel*. And now that I'm so old, they also think I'm the witch."

"Oh, no," we protested together. "No one would think you're a witch," I said.

"You don't look mean enough," Samuel added.

"You children haven't learned this yet, but frightened people don't think straight. That's what makes them dangerous." As we stepped out into the bright sunlight she concluded the discussion. "But don't think that would have kept me home. After hearing Mr. Thomas, I would have gone out to vote if it meant calling the police to come and take me in the paddy wagon."

It was hard for me to slow my steps so that we wouldn't hurry Mrs. Morris, and harder still for Samuel. Several times I had to reach behind her to tug on the end of his jacket. Each time he understood and slowed down, only to gradually speed up. Fortunately it was not far to McKinley School, where Mrs. Morris voted. As we were leaving Papa met us at the corner. He glanced at our list, suggested other names, and insisted he would drive Mrs. Morris home. Samuel and I watched him gently help her into the old De Soto and drive away before we decided whom to see next.

When we needed more names, we called Mr. Feldman's house. By suppertime I had walked what seemed a hundred miles and given a hundred arguments why voters should support Mr. Thomas and my father. Somehow Mama had managed to cook dinner between phone calls, and the three of us waited for Papa in the kitchen, sniffing good smells. When he walked in, we forgot about food and wanted to know what he'd seen and heard that day.

"I went from one polling place to the next. Then maybe back to the first. Each time I tried to decide from the face, 'Did he vote for the Socialists?' "

"What did you think, Pa? Did they?" Samuel asked.

"I decided you can't tell from looks. But soon we'll know for sure. Right after I eat, I'll go to headquarters, and we'll find out."

"Can we go with you?" I asked.

"Why not? You worked like regular party members."

Socialist headquarters for the election was Ed Feldman's house on a dead end off Broadway. The Crawley property, whose gatehouse it was that Mrs. Morris had come to as a bride, had been subdivided at a time when many of the Jews in town had prospered enough so that they no longer needed to live behind their stores. It was there that the Feldmans lived, in a house that was larger and more comfortable than any I visited often.

This night the living room was lined with trestle tables covered with mimeographed lists crosshatched with undecipherable abbreviations. Marcia Feldman and Buddy Grogan looked up from their papers to beckon us to help.

"Welcome, welcome," Marcia said. "Lots of work for everyone. Rebecca, could you please check my addition."

For the next two hours, as workers called in returns, we entered figures and added and compared.

When all the districts had reported, Dan Forsythe had gotten ninety-seven votes and Marty Grogan ninety-two, losing heavily in their battle to be commissioners. Mr. Thomas got one hundred and twelve votes, seventy fewer than in 1932. The big upset was Papa. He received one hundred and seventy-one votes, nearly a thousand fewer than Jim Tucker, but more than any other Socialist candidate. Samuel and I kissed and hugged him when the final results were called out. Everyone else in the room crowded around to shake his hand.

"My friends," Papa boomed in the tones of Franklin D. Roosevelt. Everyone laughed. Papa paused, saw we all were listening carefully, said, "I thank you," in his own voice, and sat down. More laughter and applause.

"All those months of work, and so few votes," said Mama.

"If all we wanted was to win, we could have worked for Mr. Roosevelt," Papa told her. "But look what we did instead. Because of Meyer Levine—and all his friends and family who helped, of course—fifty-nine people who probably never thought they could do such a thing voted for a Socialist. Maybe times are finally changing."

But nothing had changed at the Smart Set. "Ah-ha, the sheriff's daughter comes back to us," Mr. Goldstein said as I hung up my coat. "We were busy yesterday. You have plenty to do today to catch up."

I sat right down so that he would not see the tears I was trying to keep back and opened the big ledger so that he would stop talking to me. When I thought I could speak without my voice shaking, I said something that had been on my mind for a long time. "I don't like it when you call me 'the sheriff's daughter.' You're making fun of Papa, and that's not right. He's a good man." My voice sounded funny to me, but once I had started, I wanted to finish. "And he got even more votes than Mr. Thomas." Then I had to stop, for the tears were out, and I had to turn my back completely to hide them.

"But that was yesterday. Today the election is over and the sales have to be entered. You be sure you finish before you go to lunch—Rebecca."

However, all the tallies from the election were not yet in. Samuel had promised that after the election he would tell me who had beaten him up, and I was determined not to let him forget.

Samuel had not come in to dinner when I got home from the Smart Set, though Mama told me that he and Heshie had left their books after school and disappeared. We were in the kitchen when I heard steps on the porch. In a minute he was standing in the dining room doorway, facing the rest of us across the room.

"This is getting to be a regular thing. We sit down and you come in looking like Jack Dempsey after the big fight," Papa said, watching him closely.

"What happened this time?" Mama's tone was resigned more than frightened, for not only was Samuel hardly bruised, but he was grinning broadly.

"Not Jack Dempsey, Pa. Gene Tunney. This time I beat him."

"Beat who? Who was it? You said after the election you would tell me."

"Maybe you should tell all of us and tell us everything. Things we didn't hear before maybe," Papa said.

"That other time when I got beat up. It wasn't just kids having a fight. It was Buddy Tucker who came after me. I knew he was afraid you might win and take the job away from his father. And I decided it would make it harder for you, if you had any chance at all, if I got back at him before the election."

"All right, sit down and eat while you finish the story," said Mama. "As long as you're not hurt why should we let good food get cold?" Once we were seated, I knew Samuel would be close enough for her to get a good look at his bruises.

(99)

"After school Heshie and I went to the Tuckers'. I told Mrs. Tucker I wanted to see Buddy. Heshie just came in case he had a friend this time too. He didn't. We invited him back behind the garage and I lit into him. He wasn't frightened anymore because his father got reelected yesterday. But I remembered how much he hurt me. So I got in a few good ones and he hit me once or twice. When I left him, he was sitting down, and I think he didn't want to get up so fast."

"You didn't hurt him bad?" Mama asked.

"Mama, he weighs twenty pounds more than I do and is on the football team. I knocked him down because I was mad that two of them jumped me, but it would take three like me to do any permanent damage to him."

"Well, now the politics is over, maybe the fighting can be too. And we can go back to meals where everyone comes in all in one piece," Mama said.

Chapter 9

After the election, days at the Smart Set were longer than ever. Answers to my letters to Max came even more slowly than before. I felt as though I were leading a slow-motion life, with everything happening under a film of something dark and bad-tasting, like molasses. We were settling into a Forgetown winter, with no bright news ahead, and I wondered what would enable me to keep on getting up to one bleak day after another.

One night, almost two weeks after we said good-bye at the polls, Mrs. Morris phoned me. "Could you come to have supper with me tomorrow night? If your mother doesn't need you at home?"

"Oh, no, they don't need me. I'd love to come."

Mama was not prepared to let me go empty-handed. "You go to someone's to dinner, you must bring something. I'll bake an apple pie and I'll bring it to the store about four o'clock. It'll be just right for dinner."

"But, Ma, what if Mrs. Morris makes something else for dessert."

"She doesn't look to me like somebody who makes desserts. Store cake she'll probably serve."

Mrs. Morris thanked me for the pie, but seemed to be troubled by it. At the end of a meal of cold cuts laid out with fans of parsley and rings of hard-boiled egg slices, I saw why the pie was a problem. Mrs. Morris brought out sand-colored meringue clouds filled with vanilla ice cream.

"I don't think these will keep, that's why I'm not serving your mother's pie. You saw, I'm not much of a cook. But I did learn to make one fancy dessert. I always made it for any special event. I haven't for years." She served the meringues from a round silver tray with a filigree border that looked like lace. "But don't let that make you swell-headed," she added briskly. How sad, I thought, that the visit of an eighteen-year-old bookkeeper should be an event in the life of someone as alert as Mrs. Morris. How awful to be alone and old.

"It's delicious," I told her, letting the crisp meringue float coolly down my throat on a river of melted ice cream. "I can eat Mama's apple pie any time."

After dinner we started to talk. Rather, I listened while Mrs. Morris explained her theories about the significance of the election. It was eleven o'clock, and I had begun to wish I knew more about economics and political theory, but I had to get ready to leave. While we waited for Samuel to stop by for me on his way home from Heshie's, we drank strong tea, ate large wedges of Mama's apple pie, and agreed that I would come again the following Wednesday.

My dinners at Mrs. Morris's became small peaks between the ends of my weeks. Mama wished that I had "someone more interesting," by which she meant Jewish boys my own age, to see in the evening. But there were still not enough of them to go around.

Everything about being young, feeling alive, hoping for future joy, revolved around Max. Just thinking of Max woke parts of me that otherwise seemed only half alive. He had not been back to Forgetown since the graduation dance but he had written, telling me of the summer days behind the counter in his father's store and the nights on the Coney Island boardwalk.

Between these words I read a sweetness like the taste of strawberry jam on his lips. I felt that *Rebecca* to him, like *Max* to me, brought the scent of a spring night and the feel of it against our bodies, cool outside, but warm within.

November brought cold rains and soaring leaves, and wastepapers whipped up from the riverside. I endured each day for six o'clock and home, with the hope of a letter waiting at the top of the stairs. Weeknights, when no letter was there, were not so bad. I could think, *tomorrow*, and give away another day to buy six o'clock. A Saturday without a letter was disastrous. No mail until Monday. No plans for Saturday night. The fifty-six hours before I could hope to see a letter had to be lived by burrowing deeply into whatever novel I was reading, and shelving Rebecca Levine until Monday.

(103)

Thanksgiving passed with autumn days hurrying to winter. Evenings without mail stretched to almost a month. When six o'clock came on the Monday in December that was the darkest day of the year, Papa and I walked home quickly to the warmth of Mama's kitchen, pushed up the last stretch of hill by the wind from the river.

The familiar uneven script on the envelope was the first thing I saw as I entered the hall. "I'm going up to get washed," I called in to Mama, without entering the kitchen. I grabbed my letter and ran up to my room. The words were coldly formal; the message, the kind you write to a middle-aged aunt when your mother has said, "Poor Aunt ———. Her days are all the same with Uncle sick. Why don't you write and tell her what you're doing at school?" A list of his courses, with a brief description of each professor. The college catalogs I had read the previous spring in the assistant principal's office told me more than Max's letter. The tears streaming down my cheeks fell in a cascade on the paper in my lap. I struggled to keep from sobbing, for anyone coming upstairs to the bathroom had to pass my bedroom door. I opened my window, hoping for some noise in the street to drown out the sound of my unhappiness. But it was dinnertime, and the silent street offered no cover.

By now the river of tears over Max had been swelled by ones for Mrs. Goldstein's glinty looks, the graffiti on the sidewalk, Samuel's beating, the lost election. Sitting on the windowledge, I drew deep breaths to stop my sobs, but they fought to come back. Finally Mama's insistent "Rebecca, I'm ready with supper" stilled them. In the bathroom I scrubbed my face hard, hoping to draw attention from my bloodshot eyes and puffy nose by cheeks rubbed red. I only succeeded in adding new blotches to my well-marked face.

"Rebecca. Rebeccaaa" rang up the stairs again.

"I'm coming, I'm coming."

"Something wrong?" Samuel evaluated my efforts at disguise.

"None of your business," I answered, steadying my voice by scarcely opening my mouth.

"She's right," Papa told Samuel. "Even if she didn't tell you nice. Rebecca's upset. And whatever bothers her, if she wants to, she'll tell us. Otherwise we shouldn't ask."

I was afraid to speak and nodded my head in agreement, but I couldn't stop the tears. As I ran from the kitchen I could hear Papa. "Better she should cry it out. Keep her supper warm, Sophie. Later she'll be hungry."

Finally the tears stopped, but I waited until the scrape of chairs told me that dinner was over. Mama was alone in the kitchen. I spoke carefully. "I guess I can eat now. Then you won't have pots out all night." Mama was obviously obeying Papa's injunction about not asking questions. I thought she should know. "I got a letter from Max. I got upset because the letter wasn't very friendly."

"I figured that's what the trouble was. Wait. The next will be better."

I shook my head and continued eating. I had said all I planned. I did not want Mama to make me talk and loosen the stopper that held back the tears.

Samuel left for Heshie's. Papa went out to a meeting.

Mama took out her mending. There I was. I had a book, but I knew I would not be able to follow the dance of the words across the page. I had to get out of the house. "Mama, I promised Janet that I'd go over there after supper. I won't be late."

Mama looked up from her mending. "Don't stay long. I worry when you walk around at night."

"I won't. Ten thirty at the latest."

I gave Mama a quick peck on the top of the head to make up for having lied, and grabbed my coat from the chair in the hall, where I had dropped it when I saw my letter. Outside I knew just where to go. I would go to see Abraham. I had never been to the cemetery alone at night before, but the moon was large, cutting into the blackness.

From Easton Street I could see, a block away, the lighted yellow squares cast by the Sweet Shop and the Plaza Theatre against the gray-black of the asphalt. As the spaces between the buildings grew large and menacing, I reminded myself that it was just past eight, and I was foolish to be frightened.

Inside the wall of the cemetery the big oak tree stood watch over the five rows of headstones. Abraham's was the second in the middle row. As I thought over what I wanted to tell my big brother, I pictured him. Each visit since June he had grown more to resemble Max. Now he seemed to look more like Papa, for after all he was Papa's oldest child.

I studied the stone. ABRAHAM LEVINE—BORN AUGUST 2, 1917, DIED MARCH 11, 1919. Not even two years later. So long ago. In eighteen years the letters in the stone had scarcely worn at all; they still bore their sharply chiseled serifs. I wondered what had happened to the plain pine box he had been buried in.

For the first time I thought of Abraham. Not a handsome older brother, but a baby, dead of the flu. And what must be there, in the remains of the box. Why had I never thought of that before?

There was no big brother who would listen to my troubles, who might someday help me to leave Forgetown. There was only something that must not be thought of in the ground beneath my feet. How could I have pretended for so long that I had a brother there to help me? I backed rapidly away, as though the current that had always drawn me here had been reversed by the throwing of a giant switch. I turned and ran out onto the road, back toward town. I headed for the Sweet Shop, pursued by the knowledge of what lay under the headstone.

Live people, talking and laughing, were what I needed to see. Even if I didn't know them, I wanted to look at them. If they were here with me on the twenty-first of December, 1936, on the other side of a lighted window on Easton Street, then *they* were my brothers, not Abraham in the field, behind the stone wall.

I stood for a long time in front of the Sweet Shop. No one seemed surprised, for as long as the temperature was above freezing, kids met in, drifted away from, and returned to the lighted square. When I had calmed down, I headed home.

On Wednesday the ice cream-filled meringue shells tasted like wet cotton wool. "You aren't eating yours, Rebecca," Mrs. Morris said. "Isn't it good?"

I started to say, "It's delicious, as usual," but my voice came out a croak as tears rolled down my cheeks.

"When someone your age can't eat, it must be love. At my age, it's indigestion."

"I'm afraid I don't have a handkerchief."

"Use the napkin, it's paper. A wonderful invention. Don't let anyone tell you that all progress is bad. Some things *do* make life easier." Mrs. Morris, who loved to talk, now launched on a detailed description of all the ways in which life was now pleasanter for the housewife than when she had been a bride. I knew she was giving me time to get hold of myself, but I wanted to tell her about Max, to breathe new life in the old dreams for a few minutes. As soon as she paused for breath I told her so.

"Of course I want to know, but I was being polite."

I started with the Seder and ended with the letter.

"Most of what you told me," Mrs. Morris said, "makes him sound like a charming young man, and I'm sure you feel you're in love. But I must say, he seems to have found other interests. At your age, thinking about marriage and having a family is inevitable. And you were happy to have found a young man that you know your parents approve of. But it's that awful place, the Smart Set. You just want to get out of there, and I can't blame you. It's no place for an ambitious girl. Well, the worst mistake you could make is to stay there so long that you'll marry anybody just to get out. You'd be trading one cage for another. You need to do some things for yourself, or you're going to be sorry later on—"

I interrupted. "But what's wrong with wanting a husband and children?"

"Nothing's wrong, I suppose. I think children are wonderful. The years Newton was growing up were the best Edward and I had. Poor Newton never saw many of those himself, dying while his children were still young. Now I don't even see my grandchildren very often. His wife took them home to her parents, and only brings them here for a few days after Christmas. They hardly know me. So after life is almost over, an old woman like me can wonder if a woman should have children after all. Now, understand, Rebecca: your mother could never tell you this because it sounds like she'd be saying, 'I'm sorry I had you.' But I can because I'm just a friend."

"I never imagined a life without a husband and family."

"At your age, you wouldn't. That's probably Shaw's 'life-force' at work. And without that I wouldn't think much of the race's chance for survival. But that doesn't mean you have to give up any idea of a career for yourself—and I don't mean as a bookkeeper in the Smart Set either. You can always take some time off for that family, if you're sure you want it. I know, because I've lived almost thirty of them, how long the years can be if you're left spending the money when everyone else is gone. I suppose I could be like the rest of them and wonder if the money will last. But if I run short, I'll just sell something else. Not that you get very much for anything these days. Fortunately I don't need much. But I'm getting away from what I wanted to say. It seems we spend a lot of time worrying about the wrong things. Worry if the time is going to last, if you want to worry about something. That way you spend more time thinking about what you really want to do and going out and doing it."

"But how can I do what I want to do? What good would it do if I said I wanted to be an economist and learn about what makes hard times like this and what people can do not to have them happen? Would it do any good? Would it? If my parents need the money I make to live on?"

"Rebecca, I've known your father a long time, and let me tell you one thing. He's going to manage to take care of himself. And from what I hear about your brother, he's going to be all right too. So make up your mind. If you stay at the Smart Set, the big sacrifice you're making isn't so your family won't starve. You'll only be doing it because you're too lazy or stupid to find out if there is something else you could be doing. Don't think blaming it on other people or hard times is going to get you by. With me anyway."

By then I had stopped crying completely. The napkin was a soggy lump in my hand. I looked about for a place to put it.

"Right on your plate is all right. The best thing to do with old tears is to throw them out. That way you're reminded just how useless they are."

"I guess I won't have to cry about Max anymore."

"I hope you really mean that. It's the first step in the right direction. Now, let's get down to business. We need a list of colleges you can apply to. Some of them will have scholarships. The way to begin is to write for catalogs."

"Can I have them sent here? I think I would rather not say anything at home unless I think there is a real chance for me to go."

"You mean you're afraid your parents won't approve, don't you?"

"Isn't it ever all right to pretend something is one way, even if you don't believe it, because it makes things easier?"

"It's never all right to fool yourself. Other people, yes, if it spares their feelings. But yourself, never. It's just sloppy thinking to let yourself get away with anything. So the first rule, the very first one, is to understand what you're really doing all the time."

I walked home with Samuel, who did not push conversation on me. He must have thought that I was still unhappy about Max. Instead, I was happier than I had been since I watched Max ride away. Mrs. Morris had shown me that I could expect more from life than the Smart Set. And that I didn't have to wait for anyone to rescue me. I could do it myself.

Toward the end of January, a beaming Mrs. Morris met me at the door on my Wednesday evening. "Two came," she said, waving brown manila envelopes before my face, as I sat on a chair in her hall removing my galoshes. "Two. We'll have our work cut out for us after dinner to read through both."

But we did read through both, and then through more and more as weeks passed. My head was full of leaf-shaded campuses veined with winding paths between weathered brick buildings turning pink at sunset. I was grateful, finally, that I had not let good sense deter me from the first decision I had ever made against adult advice.

The assistant principal had not wanted to let me spend my lunch hours during my senior year in a biology class. I was able to convince him by arguing that my nearly straight-A average meant that I would surely pass. The dream which had made it possible for me to do extra classwork while working at the Smart Set, returned to lighten the needle-spray coldness of January near the river.

On Wednesdays Mrs. Morris and I argued the relative merits of this school or that, our conversations eclipsing the weather and the troubles around us. The first days of April should have brought green hopes. Instead, the spring rains brought forth a new obstacle.

I read the fine print in the catalogs. In sections labeled TUITION AND FEES ten, fifteen, or even twenty-five dollars was listed as the amount needed to accompany each application. But at the Smart Set ten dollars was all I earned for a full week's work. How could I even think about going to a college when I had no idea how I could pay the fee to apply?

"It's impossible," I said as I entered Mrs. Morris's one Wednesday. "Do you know how long it will take me to save enough to apply to just one college?"

"I've been thinking. I'm going to lend you the money you need," she answered. "What's a friend for if she can't help out?"

"I can't let you. That money would be just the beginning. There would always be something else that we hadn't thought of. I'm not giving up. But I'm not applying to any of these schools. I hope you don't think I've just wasted your time."

"That's what I tried to tell you before about time. You have to arrange it when you're young, if you want to have the time count for anything when you're old. If you say you won't apply to these schools, I can't make you. We can stop talking about college for a while, and think about something else."

We sat down to our dinner and tried to remember what we had talked about before. Certainly we had explored many subjects before the night when Max's letter told me he had turned away.

I had not forgotten Max nor his strawberry kisses, his curly hair, and my warm stirrings when he touched me. But he had slipped into the background where he, like the music in the movies, remained to be both heard and ignored. I had spent a winter fantasizing an exciting life of my own. Now spring finally had come to Forgetown. Everything was waking up, but for me another dream had died. No long talks in a professor's study, sipping sherry from fragile glasses; no shaded walks; no all-night intellectual arguments. I could feel the tears, but I knew Mrs. Morris was as lost as I without our common dream, and pushed them away.

Instead of drinking coffee from a tiny cup, I concentrated as she told me of a discussion with Norman Thomas when her son was in grade school. She and Mr.

Thomas had speculated about the world Newton's generation would know. We both carefully avoided saying that twenty-five years later Mr. Thomas was still asking for the same changes.

The doorbell rang as we searched, over ecru lace on the polished cherry table, for further conversation. It was Samuel, whom we had not expected until eleven.

"Ma called me at Heshie's and asked me to come for you."

"Is she all right?" I asked, panic draining the will even to put down my fork. "Papa?"

"Yes. It's not them. But something's wrong at the Somersets'. Their neighbor called Mama. She heard funny noises from their house since supper, then Janet ran over with our number on a piece of paper and asked her to call you to come."

"I have to go," I said to Mrs. Morris. "Samuel will walk with me."

"Of course. Next Wednesday?"

"I'll be here."

The Somersets' house looked all right. A single light burned behind the curtains in the front window. Janet answered the bell herself. I waved Samuel home. His presence might add embarassment to the pain that had made Janet send for me in the dark, through so many strangers.

"Please come in, Rebecca," she said carefully. Tears that she didn't seem to know were there rolled down her cheeks. "My father's . . . dead, and I don't know what to do about my mother. The doctor gave her something to make her sleep," she said as soon as the door closed

(114)

behind Samuel. "But she won't lie down. She keeps saying, 'Not in that bed, not in that bed.' I can't think anymore."

"Where is she?" The single light outlined the big bed in the corner of the living room. The sofa, chairs, and tables stood away from it in an ill-formed semicircle, like sensation-seekers waved back by the police from the victim of a traffic accident.

"In the kitchen. Just sitting at the table. I made her some tea, but she hasn't touched it." Janet led me between the high-armed sofa and the unfinished back of the bed.

I don't think she knew that as she talked she kept jabbing toward it with her shoulder. "We were doing the supper dishes. It was the loudest noise I ever heard."

She ignored the gasps that were breaking the flow of her words. "I was the first one in. . . . I took her back to the kitchen and she hasn't left it since. . . . The doctor told her not to look. . . . It's Doctor Whitney. . . . He went to high school with Daddy. . . . He tried to get me to stop looking too. . . ."

Janet sat finally, pulling me with her onto the sofa. I held on to her clenched fist. It was cold and damp, but unwound slightly as my fingers touched it. She drew a breath and wiped her face. "Doctor Whitney said it must have been an accident while Daddy was cleaning his gun. He said it twice. The second time was while he was putting on his coat. 'Remember. He had an accident while he was cleaning his gun.' "

"Janet, where are you?" asked a frightened voice from the kitchen.

(115)

"In the living room, Mommy, I'll be right in," Janet called toward the kitchen but kept looking at me.

"An ambulance came and took Daddy away. Doctor Whitney must have told them to take the pillows too. . . . There's hardly any . . . blood . . . on the mattress. But she says she won't sleep there."

"Could you sleep on this?" We looked down at the shiny blue damask surface of the sofa. Janet nodded. "Then make up your bed for your mother. Maybe she'll be able to sleep easier if you don't say I'm here."

Janet groped through the darkened dining room to the line of light at the bottom of the kitchen door. I hoped there would be something to help her sleep too. The sofa cushions, uncomfortable even to sit on, would be almost impossible for sleeping. As I waited for my friend the overhanging headboard seemed to edge backward toward the sofa.

"We have to get rid of this," I told her, pointing to the bed.

"But how? Who can we get to move it?"

"Us."

"But it's enormous. When Daddy brought it down, he had a terrible time. Even with two of us to help."

"We can take it apart. I've watched Papa and Samuel do it. And carry it up piece by piece. Soon it will be warm enough to sleep upstairs. Tomorrow people will come, and you don't want them to see the bed."

"I'm so ashamed. That was one of the first things I thought of. Not my Daddy, and how terrible it was, but how I was going to feel if everyone saw the bed. Even Dr. Whitney acted surprised and tried not to show it. I think Daddy would like it though, if he knew that people won't see it. He always hated having it here."

First we pulled the shades to the sill behind the net curtains. In the morning neighbors would come, hiding their inquiring eyes behind platters of food. Tonight I wanted privacy to help Janet get ready for them.

The bed had been stripped of linen. I forced myself to forget what the large bath towel hid.

"Do you think," Janet asked as we pulled at the side panels to free them from the headboard, "that he—that it happened on the bed because he hated it so much?"

"I think it will be good for you and your mother both to have it gone before morning. So we'd better keep moving."

As I had hoped the pieces grudgingly allowed themselves to be separated. Once that was done, none was too large or heavy. The metal spring, which had to be led carefully around the bend in the stairs so that we did not tear the wallpaper, gave us the most trouble.

By midnight the room was a parlor again. Before we could sit down to admire our work, the doorbell rang. Samuel looked inquiringly at Janet from the doorway.

"Come in," she told him. "Rebecca just has to put on her coat."

I saw that Janet had not thought out what she was going to say. Instead I said, "Mr. Somerset had a terrible accident." I could barely say it, and I wondered if Janet ever would be able to. "His shotgun went off while he was cleaning it and killed him. I've been helping Janet get her mother settled."

"I'm sorry," Samuel said, facing Janet with everything

(117)

but his eyes. I hugged Janet and promised to be back right after work the following day.

"She doesn't seem to be very upset," Samuel said, "for someone whose father just died."

"That's because she had to take charge. Her mother went to pieces. Janet had to do everything, with nobody but me to help."

The rest of the way home Samuel and I hardly spoke. I tried to imagine how I might feel if Papa died. No one in our house would laugh much without him. Each night at dinner Papa was our court jester, entertaining us with stories. His day was full of people. He brought home a scent of life in the world outside that helped Mama, alone at home, and me, alone in my office at the store, to see humor in our days.

I shivered, and shook my head in disbelief that one minute someone I loved could be next to me, laughing, talking, and then gone the next. Nothing could be counted on, could be permanent, could be always there. We had to love each other, knowing we would lose each other. We had to convince ourselves that life was better that way than if we never loved anyone at all.

Mr. Somerset was buried at eleven o'clock Friday morning from the gray stone Episcopal Church on Broadway. The church, centered in its graveyard, ended a line of small one-story houses coming up from the river. Beyond the church was a block of larger houses; then still larger ones on more land; until finally, at the top of the hill, the Wallingtons'.

The church was one of the landmarks we had passed on the way home from Mr. Thomas's speech, so sure, somehow, that things would get better. Mr. Somerset, in his solitary confinement, had not been able to wait. For over a year he had denied his existence; now he had completed the obliteration.

At breakfast Friday Papa asked what time the funeral was to be held. "I'll close the shop at a quarter of," he told me, "and come by for you."

As I waited outside the Smart Set, I pictured Papa in his neat dark suit and the homburg he so carefully cleaned and put away at the end of each season, pulling down the shades in the windows of his shop and hanging the sign on the door. Then quickly he was at my side, offering his arm for the walk up Broadway.

"How come you decided to come with me, Pa? You never met Mr. Somerset."

"Janet is your friend. How many times has she been at our house? How would it look if your father couldn't take half an hour to pay respects? I'm so busy with business maybe?"

"I'm happy I don't have to go alone. And I don't think there'll be many people there."

Janet and Mrs. Somerset sat in the first row. Janet's sister had not been able to travel from Phoenix because of the expense. Fewer than two dozen people sat in tiny islands in the pews. I led Papa to the second pew. I wanted Janet to know we were there. I was sure she would sense my presence if we sat close enough.

To the right of the altar an easel held a single wreath of lilies. Mrs. Somerset and Janet, I thought. I wondered how long it had been since Janet's mother had bought flowers. Hers was the first house I had known that had flowers in the winter. They used to stand in a pitcher of rose-colored glass on a low table in front of the sofa—large creamy white chrysanthemums with dark glossy leaves. The table was the first piece of furniture we put back in place after we carried the bed upstairs.

The organ played what I supposed must be hymns; I occasionally recognized one we had sung in school. Then, the minister spoke, his voice seeming an extension of the rolling tones of the organ, which took up again when he stopped. After he finished, he walked down the center aisle. Four men in dark suits with striped trousers picked up the coffin, large and polished, flashed with metal at the ends. Janet and her mother came next. Papa and I walked out behind them, the others in the church waiting at the ends of their rows to fall into line.

In the cemetery a low wrought-iron fence set off a large plot with few headstones. How comfortable for the living, I thought. We don't even call them burying grounds. Instead, we lay out the places for the dead, each with a room of his own, families together as though still in their homes.

The coffin was set next to the freshly dug grave. The minister opened his prayer book. "Dust to dust, earth to earth." He reached down for a handful of dirt, rich and black, as though ready for the spring. We all, except Papa, recited the Lord's Prayer. A short blessing. Then the minister was at Mrs. Somerset's side, leading her away from the grave as he spoke. I was glad Janet would not have to watch her father's coffin being lowered into the ground.

I remembered the funeral of Tanta Greenbaum's father, when his wife, a tiny old woman, broke away from
Tanta's arm to fall to her knees at the edge of the grave
and call to the coffin below, "*Sholem, Sholem. Geh nit
avec.*" Don't go away. This was easier; to leave with the
casket still next to the grave.

"Papa, I told Mr. Goldstein I wouldn't be back until
after lunch. I want to see if I can help Janet at home." I
kissed Papa's cheek and watched him, jaunty in his good
suit and hat, as he headed down the hill toward Easton
Street. Except for Papa, only women—one here, two
there—had been at the service.

Had Mr. Somerset died while the Works was still
operating, it would have been closed for the morning.
Rows of workmen in stolid navy blue would have ab-
sorbed the echoes of the voice and the music, asserting
life in the empty nave. Today, none. Were they working
at other factories where they dared not ask for a few
hours off? Were they hiding out in some distant shanty-
town? Or were they sitting behind genteel lace curtains,
sending their wives and daughters to represent them?

I watched Janet and her mother being helped into a
long black limousine. "I'll see you back at the house," I
mouthed as Janet turned toward me and then started
slowly down Broadway. Guiltily I realized I was enjoying
myself. I was having a day off in the middle of the week.
I knew Janet would like to see me as soon as possible,
but I couldn't hurry. The wind was blowing away the
smell of cheap rayon that leaked from the boxes of blouses
and slips and brassieres in the Smart Set. For a few hours

I was away from the half-glass partition and the eye of Mrs. Goldstein.

For the first time I thought of Mr. Somerset. Was he dead because he could never be outside on a day like this, but only watched it from the other side of the glass? Did he forget how it felt to breathe such a day? To smell it, to share with the magnolia and dogwood the long-awaited arrival of spring?

Was that how it was possible for him to lie down for the last time on a hated bed and pull the trigger that meant no more? Because he had been so long inside his house that he had forgotten how beautiful the outdoors could be? Would that happen to me if I stayed at the Smart Set? Would viewing the world through the half glass mean half seeing at first, not seeing at last?

I turned on Easton and saw the Works for the first time since the weather had turned. Ordinarily I managed to hurry into the Smart Set without looking toward the river. *That's where Mr. Somerset should be buried,* I thought. *That's where he died.* Under the hard-packed earth in the yard beyond the lacy fence. Beneath the windows, gap-toothed with broken panes. The debris, carried there by the winds of two winters, tossed there with scorn by passers-by, could be picked up, piece by piece. Everyone in Forgetown could take away one sheet of newspaper or a soaked cardboard carton or an empty bottle. A patch could be cleared, and now, as the earth was beginning to thaw, he could be buried there as a reminder that a man is dead if his world has no place for him.

"Only so few people? They lived here so many years,

and only so few people?" Mama echoed my thoughts as Papa and I reported the funeral at dinner.

"What difference can it make to him how many people came to his funeral?" Samuel asked.

"It's for the family," Mama insisted. "It's to show respect for the family. How much a person was thought of."

"Bourgeois frills," Samuel commented. Then, turning to me: "I thought you said Janet's father had a job in Panama."

"I guess he was home for a while and I didn't hear about it."

"Cleaning a gun seems to be a funny thing to do if you're just home for a visit," he persisted.

"People who are foolish enough to have guns are foolish enough to clean them any time they feel like," Mama said, dismissing the subject.

Papa remembered an important point. "Now we all have one less friend," he said slowly. "Rebecca always said how nice he was to her and how he always asked about her family."

One less friend. Papa's words came back to me as I waited for sleep. Mr. Somerset bowing over my hand and saying, "I trust your mother is well, Rebecca." How long ago had that been? A year and a half, at least. Near the end, had Mr. Somerset been so polite? Had he kept his old-fashioned courtesies? Had he put pillows behind his head with unswerving southern good manners, so that his wife and daughter would have an easier job of cleaning up?

Saturday afternoon Janet and her mother were alone. The neighbors, who had helped the day before, had now gone back to their own lives. Janet led me to the kitchen, where Mrs. Somerset was scooping up papers to snap them back into a metal strongbox. Janet stopped her. "It's all right, Mommy, Rebecca can see." She handed me a paper closely covered with typescript. "I think this is a paid-up life insurance policy. What do you think, Rebecca?"

I took my time reading it to be sure. "I think so too," I finally agreed.

"It seems to be a thousand-dollar twenty-payment life insurance policy."

"A thousand dollars," Mrs. Somerset said. "He must have finished paying for it just before he lost his job."

"Do you think he forgot he had it?" Janet asked.

As soon as I realized that Janet would get some money from this paper, I knew that would be the question she would ask. "If he never mentioned it to either of you, then he must have forgotten."

"You see, Mommy, it's the way I said. He finished paying for it long ago and then just forgot about it. If he had remembered, he would have said something when he borrowed against the other policy, or later, before the—accident." The pause before the last word was scarcely noticeable, as though she was beginning to accept it. Now it was even more important that she believe that her father had not taken his own life.

"That's so much money," I said.

"When I was married, we went on a six-month honeymoon and spent twice that. But that was before the Great

(124)

War. Everything was different then. Now a family could live for two years on that. Two years."

"Two years," Janet echoed. "If we don't spend any money on anything. We can scrape by just like we have. . . ." Her glance seemed to expose the army cot behind the door to the cellar, the pantry empty except for scattered cans of beans and some macaroni.

"But we'll have the roof over our heads, and as long as we pay our taxes . . ."

Two years of the scarcities revealed by Janet's look seemed a poor exchange for her father's life; but neither she nor I could say so. I hoped that at least her mother would never see it that way.

"Janet," Mrs. Somerset said, "we shouldn't discuss our finances with our friends. It was good of Rebecca to come to see you. It's nice out. Why don't you two go for a walk?"

Once outside Janet immediately turned to me. "It was left to her. I'm a minor and can't do a thing. She's going to use it up, ten dollars a week, just like the money in the bank. It's all right for her. She's old. She just has to keep on getting by. . . . But what about me? She's telling me I have to stay at the five-and-ten so she can have her house and pretend everything is the way it was before we lost our money."

"What else could you do?"

"We could sell the house, or rent it. And I could use the money to go to secretarial school. I know I could get a better job, and we could live a little better. But she says it's a gamble, and if I didn't get another job after I finished, we'd be even worse off."

"It's a lot of money. When you think that it could feed you for two years—"

"Two more years like this, you mean. All I do is work and walk home, the same as you. We don't even have anything to talk about, you and I. Or wouldn't if the accident hadn't happened."

"So you noticed too."

Janet stopped and held her hand out so I would not go on. "You see? Even we forget that we have feelings and brains. We're just machines to bring home money that's not quite enough to keep us alive. And never any for buying something pretty or doing something silly."

"Where should we walk?" I asked. Janet was saying things it hurt too much to hear, asking questions I had circled for months.

"Anyplace but downtown. I don't even want to see that store," she said. "I wake up in the morning and first thing, I think, 'Good, I don't have to go to work,' and then I remember why I'm on the sofa and what's happened. Then I'm angry that I was happy."

So we snaked through the streets above Easton Street, working our way out onto Broadway, far enough beyond the church so that Janet did not have to acknowledge the graveyard. The Wallingtons' house rose above us. As a distraction I described for her again the night of the meeting.

Now the afternoon sun, glancing off it, brightened the house that had seemed gray and dirty the last few times that I had passed. Calmly it sat on its hilltop, evaluating the activities of the town.

Monday night at the dinner table Papa surprised me

by mentioning it. "Celia Wallington came into the store today to say good-bye. The doctor told her husband that he shouldn't be here, where all the time he sees the Works and what happened to it. So they are going to sell the house and move to the seashore. There they have a house they used to go to in the summer."

"Leave that beautiful house?" I forgot that it had begun to seem a bit shabby and remembered the creamy smoothness of the marble mantel, the dark, shiny floors, the velvet flowers on the wallpaper.

"Wherever she lives will be nice, don't you worry." Mama said. "A lady like Mrs. Wallington wouldn't live anyplace, it wasn't fixed up."

Samuel asked an important question. "Who would buy that house? It must cost a mint to heat it."

"That I couldn't ask," Papa told him. "I wished her good luck, and she said she wanted me to know that she would still come twice a year and stay with her sister so I could make her a suit. She should live and be well and come once a year, I would be satisfied."

I had spoken to Mrs. Wallington only once in my life. Before and after that I had seen her many times as she hurried along Broadway. But the thought of the Wallingtons leaving Forgetown, of their house being boarded up like the Works . . .

Now I would have to avoid upper Broadway too. The rot would be eating at the sound buildings and pleasant streets from two directions. Would each week mark off new streets where I did not wish to walk until I would be locked in the path from my house to the store?

Chapter 10

The funeral seemed to have been the first and last day of spring; cold, gray days followed. On one such Thursday I came out of the Smart Set to find Heshie waiting for me. Without thinking, I looked behind him for Samuel. In response he peered over my shoulder and asked, "Is this the newest way to say hello? Not to the person you see, but to someone you don't?"

"I'm sorry, but I sort of expected to see my brother."

"Well, he's not here. Just me. I came to walk you home. Okay?"

"I'd love the company. But what's the occasion?"

"I just wanted to, that's all."

When I asked him how things were going at school, his eyes slid toward me, but he did not face around. "I guess you'll have to know sometime," he said. "Samuel and I hardly go anymore."

"How could that be? The school hasn't said anything. The truant officer—"

"Maybe because it's near the end of the year. Or they're busy with other kids. But I'm not going back next year. Samuel says he won't either. I'm nearly eighteen. I know what I want and I won't get it in school."

I had forgotten that Heshie was older than Samuel by almost a year. "What *do* you want?" I asked.

"I'm good at business even though I'm not good at schoolwork. I know ways to make money. And I know the business I want to go into."

"Not your father's?"

"No. Sitting and waiting for people to need whiskey so bad they'll spend food money is not for me."

I turned to face Heshie. All the Greenspans looked alike: tall, big-boned, fair-haired, with large regular features. I was always surprised at the resemblances, even between his mother and his father. Heshie was a good-looking boy. As we walked up the street I thought we made a handsome couple. Of course I would not tell him so, and asked instead, "What do you want to do then, instead of school?"

"It's still sort of secret, with me and Samuel, so you'll have to promise. Though nothing your father would say now would stop us. We kept our part of the bargain. We stayed in school this year."

"I promise then. Unless you're planning to rob a bank, I mean. Then I would tell him, promise or no promise."

"No banks. Besides, that's not the kind of thing you tell someone, even if they promise."

"Of course."

"We think we can buy the movie theater in New Vernon. Not the big one, the Palace, but the Strand, off Main Street."

"You've been drinking. Let me smell your breath. Buy a theater? You must be crazy."

"It's not crazy. I talked to Mr. Richardson in the bank. They foreclosed the theater and shut it down six months ago. He knows they'll never get any money out of it unless they get it running again and—"

I interrupted him. "You talked to Mr. Richardson? At the bank?"

"I did. And he let me talk. He even said they might let us run the theater and pay them their money as we earn it."

"Two kids like you and Samuel, who haven't even finished high school. What could you run?"

"We ran our lawn-cutting business."

"Cutting a few lawns is no business." I sounded like Mama.

"Maybe not. But we'll both be good at this. We both even passed bookkeeping. As long as I don't have to talk French, people'll never know whether I graduated or not."

"It isn't only French. What do you know?"

"About the movies, lots. What makes people laugh, which stars they like to see. We can tell who will fill a theater better than the people who run them now."

"It still sounds like a pipe dream. When are you going to tell my father?"

"As soon as the bank is ready to tell us what kind of guarantees they want. Then my father and yours will have to come with us to talk to them."

"I guess Papa will go. If it's what Samuel wants."

"He does. He's sure, like I am." We had turned the last corner. "But what I wanted to talk to you about is Saturday night. Would you like to see *Mary of Scotland* with me?"

I thought for a minute. I had not had a date since the Senior Prom. Each Saturday night seemed longer than the last. Walking up Easton Street beside Heshie felt good.

"I'd like to," I told him.

His answer surprised me. "I always thought Katharine Hepburn looked like you, a little."

Heshie was rapidly graduating from being just my brother's friend. He left me at the bottom of the steps, saying he had to hurry but, I suspected, not wishing to see anyone in my family. "Half past seven on Saturday all right?" he asked. "We can take the quarter-of bus."

"I'll be ready." Going up the two dozen steps I improvised a Fred Astaire routine, without once thinking that dancing was inappropriate for a high school graduate of serious intentions who was the head bookkeeper of a prosperous business.

The only dress I had to wear on Saturday was the one I wore two days a week to work, alternating it with a skirt paired with one of my two blouses. The first was three years old, the new one bought in September. Nothing was right for the way I felt.

In my closet, covered with an old sheet, was the graduation dress. It was April, almost May, in fact. If I wore it with the plain belt instead of the blue sash, it would not be too fancy for the movies. And perhaps I could buy a new pair of stockings, which Mrs. Goldstein would let me pay for at the rate of twenty-five cents a week.

Saturday always passed slowly at the Smart Set. This one was the slowest of them all. At last I escaped into a bright evening that hinted spring had come to stay. At home I washed my hair and did my nails with a pale pink polish that made my fingers look long.

By the time seven thirty came, I had been in and out of my white dress three times, carefully, so that I got no lipstick on the collar. Each time I took it off, I did so because it seemed too nice for the movies.

In the end I left it on. I preferred to look pretty, even though I might feel foolish, than to dress sensibly but to feel as drab and unimportant as I did on ordinary days. Heshie's eyes brightened when he saw the dress. I was grateful that neither Mama nor Samuel mentioned it. What Papa said was fine—"a good job," straightening the collar so it lay flat, "even if I say so myself."

Heshie held the heavy dark red coat that I had worn through four winters. Even though my coat hid everything underneath, I could forget how much I hated it, knowing that when it blew open, my beautiful dress would show.

My family had carefully avoided commenting about my date. I suspected that Mama had administered a sharp warning to Papa and Samuel as well as choosing her own words cautiously. Nevertheless, Heshie and I simultaneously let out our breath as we reached the sidewalk. We smiled in conspiratorial recognition as we headed for the bus stop.

Back home after the movies, just outside the ring of light cast by the streetlamp, Heshie kissed me. I had not expected he would try until we reached the porch. I was glad that he was big enough to take complete charge and leave no chance for hesitation. He kissed like a man, not like my kid brother's friend. In a way that I had not with Max, I felt like a woman, not a girl who had been kissed only four times before.

"When I saw the white dress," he said, "I knew you liked me." He had started to walk up the stairs with me. "I'd better get you in the house before your mother is out here." We could hear Mama in the hall. "I'll be here tomorrow, in the afternoon," he said, and was off down the stairs as the outside light flashed on.

I didn't bother with a greeting. "Mama, I'm eighteen and a half and have been working for over a year. I don't expect you to wait up for me every time I go to the movies."

"What you expect and what I expect don't have to be the same. I have to do what I have to do."

"Next time, at least let me open the door with my key and come in myself without flashing the light like I was some kind of a criminal."

"Who said anything about criminal? I was just trying to make it easier, you shouldn't have to fumble for your key. But if you get so upset, I won't." Pause. "Did he say anything, you know, about maybe seeing you again?"

"It's Heshie Greenspan, Ma. He spends half his life here. He'd have to wear blinders if he wasn't going to see me again." Then I felt sorry for Mama and relented. "He said he would come over in the afternoon tomorrow."

Mama nodded in approval. I hung my old coat in the downstairs closet and followed her up, still feeling pretty in the white organdy.

As I lay in bed Mama's unexpressed thoughts made me examine my feelings about Heshie. She certainly treated him as a serious suitor. His kiss had been serious too. Suddenly he had stopped being my kid brother's friend. I could still feel the pressure of his arms across my back, pulling me close.

I knew I had been happy when he said he would stop by for me on Sunday, for that would mean more kisses, more feelings that, while new, were also anticipated. My body had been awaiting them a long time and had no trouble knowing what to do now that they had started.

Sunday afternoon we walked up Broadway among the wide lawns and expensive houses. I had wondered what I would talk to Heshie about. He had read none of the books I had, and I assumed he feared none of my demons. I was surprised to find he had accurate opinions about the people we knew in common. His ideas grew out of a sharp observation of the real world, not from words on paper. I decided maybe I could learn from him.

In the woods at the top of Broadway, beyond the last house, Heshie kissed me among saplings softened with pale green buds. When his hand felt for my breast, opening the buttons of my coat, caressing me through the silkiness of my best blouse, I wanted him to stop and to not stop at the same time. I pulled back, saying I had to get home before Mama worried.

"But it's not late."

"Not late, maybe, but I'd better get home anyway. I have things to do to get ready for work."

"Would you go to the movies next Saturday again?"

"Yes, but now I want to get home."

Samuel had said nothing about my having been out with his friend, perhaps because he did not know how he felt about it. As I washed out the stockings and collars and cuffs I would need for the morning, I heard him call to Mama that he was going to Heshie's. I was happy that I was not interfering with his friendship. For one awful moment I wondered if Heshie would say anything about kissing me. Then I decided that he had been as excited and troubled as I and would not talk of it to Samuel.

Of course Monday was the same at the Smart Set. What was different were the memories of being kissed and touched and the impatience for Saturday when I would sit in the darkened theater in the circle of Heshie's arm.

On Wednesday I went as usual to Mrs. Morris's.

"You look springlike, Rebecca," she said. "It's very becoming."

Hanging up the old coat, I realized she was not referring to my clothes. My face must be showing that new feelings were waking with the spring. I wanted to talk to someone. Not Mama; although I was aware that she had once been young, I was sure that was in a time and place when everything was different.

Janet was still in mourning. I could not talk to her of buds unfolding inside while she was closed up with the death of her father. Mrs. Morris was my only other friend. She was so old as to be no age at all. She lived so much with thoughts and ideas that surely she must be able to remember, if only for a few minutes of listening or for a few sentences of approval, how it felt to be young in the spring.

I attacked my dinner as though I had not recently seen food, and as Mrs. Morris smiled I recalled her words the time when I could not eat the meringue because I had thought Max didn't care. I knew she expected me to say something. "I guess if not eating means being unhappy in love, eating with a good appetite must mean the opposite."

"I would imagine so," she answered, being careful to leave most of the questioning out of her voice.

I decided I wanted to answer the question that was there. "There is a boy—a young man. . . ."

"Is it someone you've mentioned?"

"It's not Max." I said it slowly, remembering how Max looked through the train window the last time I saw him. "But there's no need to make a mystery. It's Hershel Greenspan, Samuel's friend who comes with him sometimes to walk me home."

"I thought he was still in school."

"He is, sort of. He's not going to finish. He wants to go into business. The movie business."

"Does he know anything about it?"

"He says he does. And he's smart."

"It doesn't seem smart not to finish high school. He must be younger than you."

"He's nearly eighteen. But he's very sure of himself and what he wants."

"Are you so sure of what you want? Spring is such a

hard time for young people. Everything is waking up and they want to be part of it."

"No, it's not that," I said, suspecting it was.

"Let me finish. I never talked about this. There was no one here to tell. It's about my son, Newton. For a long time now I've thought he'd still be alive if he hadn't fallen in love and married when he did. . . . He was young too, and it was already hard times. And when they had the second child, his wife wouldn't let them live here, where they could've saved on the rent. He was working at two jobs when he got pneumonia. He was only sick ten days. They say disease travels faster in young blood."

"Oh, I'm sorry."

"No, you're not. I don't mean that the way it sounds. Why shouldn't you be a little sorry? It's a sad story. But you never knew Newton, so I can't expect it to mean much to you. But what I am trying to say is—make sure it doesn't happen to you. That you don't fall in love just because you're eighteen and it's spring."

I heard Mrs. Morris's words but they seemed addressed to someone else. They had little to do with my feelings about Heshie.

I answered the door when the bell rang at half past ten. Heshie was there to pick me up instead of Samuel. The quick leap of my blood lighted my face. I knew I wanted to avoid introductions and small talk. I motioned to him to wait on the stoop while I said good-bye to Mrs. Morris. As I hurriedly promised to come the following Wednesday I thought her smile knowing. I did not stop to find out if she had guessed that it was not Samuel who was waiting for me.

(137)

In the first darkened space between streetlights Heshie kissed me. Guilt and excitement, dark and shiny, awoke. Alarmed by my response, I invoked the need to hurry home, but happily he did not listen right away. It was past eleven when we reached our steps. The living room lights still shone in bright yellow patches that ran across the porch and down onto the steeply sloping lawn.

"That's our car." Heshie indicated the long black sedan that I had overlooked in surprise at all the lights.

"Your father's here?"

"Yep. He said he had to talk sometime to your father, and it might as well be now. Let's go see."

From the top of the stairs Samuel beckoned us up to his room. "They've been yelling at each other for an hour," he said, shutting his bedroom door behind us. "It's a draw. I think your father'll be leaving soon, if you want a ride home."

"I don't mind walking. I'll stay to hear what your father says."

We heard the door close. Papa called up the steps for Samuel. He was still angry but looked embarrassed at seeing Heshie following Samuel and me downstairs. "Your father just left. If you hurry . . ." As he spoke the engine started up sharply in the late night stillness.

"It's all right, Mr. Levine. I can walk—when we hear what happened."

"So we'll all talk. Sophie, come out of the kitchen." Mama looked as if she had been crying. Papa put his arm around her shoulder. "Don't mind what he said." Apologetically he added, looking at Heshie, "He's a *prost* man, your father. He never had a chance for much education. And he doesn't think it's important. Maybe he's right. But all my life I thought different. Now who knows? Most people would say he's better off, and I got nothing but *tsuris* from trying to educate myself all these years. Still I can't change so easy. This time I can't convince you to stay in school?" He looked first at Samuel, then at Heshie.

They shook their heads in unison.

"Only one more year," Mama pleaded.

"Not past the end of this year. Even that's more than we promised." Samuel sounded very sure of himself. But he showed me the uncertainty underneath when he added too casually, "Why stop now? We've almost finished the year."

Why not stop now, if you're convinced you'll never need it? I asked the question silently, trying to keep it from my eyes. Beneath the seeming confidence that he was doing right, Samuel was providing alternatives.

Heshie said it for me. "I want to just stop. But he says we have to finish. So we get credit for the year."

"That makes sense," I said.

"Not to me," Heshie said.

"We've been over that," Samuel told him. "It's seven weeks to the end. Let's finish. We can do both for that long."

"Both, what both?" Mama looked from Papa to Samuel to Heshie and back.

"Go to school and manage the theater we're going to be running," Samuel answered.

"I agreed, Sophie. Myron Greenspan is going to sign a

note to the bank, and I'm going to sign one for him. He says the bank doesn't want my signature, but he'll take it. Not because it's any good, he says, but because Heshie wants Samuel as a partner. Myron says my children are hard workers. He's sure he won't take a loss. A terrible embarrassment, Samuel. I only could do it because you made me believe it was very important to you."

"It is, Pa. I'm no student, and I'll be just a nobody with a high school diploma. If we can make our business go, we'll be important in town. We'll be somebody."

"Nobody can be somebody if he doesn't learn when he has the chance."

"Pa, you'll have to trust that I'm not a fool, and this is how it has to be for me."

"I'll hope, I'll hope. You know I only want what's good for you."

"I know."

"Now it's late," Mama said. "Heshie, you should go home. Rebecca and Samuel, to bed. Tomorrow is work and school."

Long after I was in bed, I heard the murmur of Mama and Papa's voices through the wall we shared. At first I wondered why my name was mentioned. Then I realized they were talking not about the theater but about my coming home with Heshie. Straining, I made out that Papa was unhappy at the thought of his daughter allied to a Greenspan: uneducated, socially unaware.

I stopped trying to listen and slid back into the events of the evening. As though from a great distance Mrs. Morris's words came back. Was I so sure of what I wanted? Heshie and Samuel seemed to be. They saw what they wanted and did what they had to to get it.

Papa and Mama were sad. That did not stop Samuel. He knew the life they had tailored for him would never fit comfortably, however much they altered it. He would have to be the one who changed. Samuel was neither ashamed of what he was, nor desirous of being anything else. But what about me? Was I wrong to go on at the Smart Set? Staying there because I helped out a little at home, marrying Heshie or someone like him, living Mama's life except that I would read a few more books?

I had always believed there must be something more than life in Forgetown. Even if I lived in a house like the Wallingtons', I would still travel the same streets, searching the familiar faces.

The books that I had been reading for half a dozen years could be wrong. Maybe nothing out there was really more exciting than Forgetown. I could throw away what was known and good and find something rotten and strange. But unless I went, I would never know.

I could stay, growing more pleased and excited with each touch and sight of Heshie, and perhaps marry him and raise handsome Greenspan children with fair hair and high-bridged noses. But Rebecca Levine would entirely disappear, cut up into pieces so small they would evaporate; adding columns in the Smart Set; eating meringues on Mrs. Morris's dining room table while the room became more and more bare as she sold her furniture; sitting around the kitchen table while Papa made us laugh with stories of his customers; eventually sharing a Greenspan or a Feldman or a Toplinsky life. If I was to hold on to Rebecca, I would have to move now.

(141)

Chapter 11

Mrs. Goldstein reluctantly let me have two hours off on the following Wednesday afternoon to keep an appointment at the high school. I told Mrs. Morris about it that night. "I can get a tuition scholarship to teachers' college if I pledge to teach for one year. The railroad has a special student rate. I can go back to working part-time at the store and make enough for my fare. I'll be able to finish in four years, and they'll help me to find my first job."

"But teaching! We never thought you'd be a teacher. . . . A lot of squirmy children who don't want to be where they are."

"I hope it doesn't mean I'll teach forever. Of course I didn't tell Mr. Crawford that. I want to teach near a university, so I can keep on going to school."

"Have you told your parents? Or—Hershel?"

I shook my head. "No one. I only applied this afternoon. I used you as a reference. Is that all right?"

"Of course."

"Mr. Crawford thought my application should be in the mail today. I'm already late. He canceled everything to help me fill out the forms. He said he was sad last year when I graduated second in the class, and then did nothing but go work at the Smart Set. And all along I never thought anyone else noticed."

I had decided that I would tell Mama and Papa of my decision over the weekend, when there would be plenty of time for talk. After that I could tell Heshie.

This time when the doorbell rang, I brought Heshie in to meet Mrs. Morris. What seemed to be a long silence followed the introduction as each examined the other. Mrs. Morris, more practiced in the social niceties, spoke first. "I'm always happy to meet a friend of Rebecca's. I consider her to be a very good friend of mine."

"I've heard a lot about you," Heshie said after another, shorter, pause.

"If you grew up anywhere near this house, you probably heard I was a witch. For a long time I used to be angry when I heard the children whisper it to each other. They were afraid if they said it out loud, I'd put them under a spell." And musingly after another wait: "And maybe I would have too."

"Our house isn't near here; it's over on the other side of town, near the Levines," Heshie answered.

"What did she mean about putting the children under a spell?" he asked me after we were out of the door.

"Oh, she was just teasing. She knows we don't believe in witches."

"Maybe *we* don't. But what about her? Don't you think she does? That's a spooky place. All those dark floors and that dark furniture and one twenty-five-watt bulb burning. I wish you didn't go there."

"She's one of my best friends. I could never have gotten through this winter without her."

While arguing about Mrs. Morris, we had walked by the place where Heshie had kissed me the week before. He found another spot between streetlights and pulled me close. I had been troubled that my friends had not liked each other, but forgot that when I felt him against me.

I decided I'd better tell him right away. I couldn't face him and mumbled to his necktie, "Today I filled out an application to teachers' college. If they accept me, I'll start in September. I won't live away from home. But I guess I'll be very busy, because I'll have to work at the store. You're the only one who knows. Don't say anything to Samuel yet."

"What about her? I bet you told her."

"Mrs. Morris is different. She's been helping me apply to colleges all winter."

"Why does she want you to go to college so much?"

"She thinks the only future for me is to have a job or a profession that will get me out of Forgetown."

"What's so bad about Forgetown?"

"Nothing's so bad. Only that she thinks the only important life is a life of ideas. I guess she would like it if I became a college professor."

"Sounds dull to me. She forgets what it's like to be young and to want more than mooning about a lot of philosophy."

"I don't think she forgets much. Only she hardly notices whether she has people around or not."

"Don't kid yourself. She knows perfectly well what people are around. I just bet that if they aren't people she's interested in, she ignores them. I hope she isn't making you that way too."

"She's not making me into anything. What I've decided to do I decided myself. I have to find out whether I can make anything of my life or not."

"A girl like you should find somebody to take care of her, not worry about crazy ideas."

"It's probably not normal, but I don't think getting married and having a lot of children is enough for a whole life."

"Most girls think it is."

"I know. That's why I said I wasn't normal. I know other girls don't feel the way I do."

Heshie looked at me carefully, as though a sign on my face or body should proclaim my strangeness. We pulled slightly apart, staying that way without talking until we got home.

I told Mama and Papa at breakfast over the half-filled cups of sweet milky coffee and the sugary crumbs of Mama's cinnamon buns that were our Saturday morning breakfast. Mama frowned. Papa came over to kiss my cheek.

"Well," he said, "at least you don't think you know everything about everything. I never thought you wanted to be a teacher, but why not? Why not? It's a good profession."

"Just watch you shouldn't be an old maid, taking care of other people's children when you could be raising your own," Mama said, indicating what was on her mind.

"Sophie, she's a young girl. How old are you, Rebecca? Eighteen and a half maybe?" I nodded. "She has plenty of time to decide when she wants children, and whose."

"She's right. She should go," said Samuel—always the last to come to meals—when he heard my news. "She's the one who belongs in school, not me."

I took a long sip of the sweet coffee, feeling it go smoothly down my throat, mingling with the warm pleasure of hearing "She's right, she's right."

Then Samuel remembered. "Did you tell Heshie?"

"Wednesday night when he walked me home. But I told him not to say anything until I told all of you."

"What did he say?" At Samuel's question Mama turned to watch me while I answered.

"What could he say? I shouldn't be thinking about a career, but I should be looking for a husband."

Mama nodded sharply in agreement. "You see. Everyone knows what's right for a girl your age."

"Sophie, maybe that was all right for you. But today, a girl, if she's ambitious, can have an education. She can have a career."

"The best career for a woman is to have a family."

"You say that because that's what you know," I said, remembering my talks with Mrs. Morris. "But maybe we're beginning to organize our society so women can do something more."

"Organize, organize. You sound like a union. Only some things don't change. It still takes nine months to make a baby and a mama and a papa to do it." Everyone was embarrassed to hear such talk from Mama.

"She's young enough, she can find out these things herself," Papa said. "It's more important that Rebecca knows what she wants to do and is doing something about it."

We went about our separate Saturdays. It was easier for me to go to the Smart Set now that I knew I would not be there forever. I planned the speech that I would use to petition Mr. Goldstein for a part-time job again, once the school accepted me.

At the end of May Heshie and Samuel started to spend their weekends at the theater. During the week they stayed in school, while a cashier looked after the Strand. Heshie no longer had time to take me with him on Saturday nights, to excite me with his mouth and hands in the darkness. Once more I was reduced to filling my Saturday nights with books.

My acceptance came just a month after the application had been filed. When Mama, who had been instructed to open any letter from the school, telephoned me with the news, I called Mrs. Morris. She made me promise to bring the letter when I came on Wednesday so she could read it herself. That night after dinner I ran to the Somersets. Janet came to the door as soon as I rang the bell.

"Come for a walk," I said. "It's beautiful out, and I have something to tell you."

"Something romantic?" She called in to her mother that we would not be gone long.

"Not very," I answered. "But exciting, I think. I've been accepted at teachers' college. I'll start in September."

"You never told me you were applying."

"I didn't tell anyone, in case I was turned down."

"Now you're going to get out of the Smart Set after all."

I was sure that Janet and I both thought then of the five-and-ten. I hadn't realized before that getting ahead meant getting ahead of someone else. I wanted to cry. I hadn't wanted to leave Janet behind. We had done things together since the second grade, measuring ourselves, one against the other. It was frightening to think of moving on without her.

"You'll find a way of getting out too," I said finally. "Maybe next year you could apply for a scholarship, too."

"Maybe" was all she said.

Janet walked next to me in the darkening night, her eyes turned straight ahead.

"I'm glad for you," she said before she ran up her porch stairs.

"Thank you," I called, wondering if I could have been as gracious as my friend if she had told me she were going to school while I was staying on in Forgetown.

School closed for summer vacation. Samuel left at noon for the theater each day, returning long after the rest of us were asleep.

One Sunday in July, when pockets of heat lingered

throughout the house and petunias drooped in their parched bed beneath the kitchen window, Heshie phoned just as we sat down to supper. He told us that Samuel had decided he must see their distributor and had caught the last train into the city. He would sleep at the Y and make his call early Monday morning. When he was done, he would take the two thirty train out of the city and go directly to the theater.

Monday found me at my ledger, behind the finger-smeared glass portion of the wall that divided my office from the rest of the store. I don't know what made me look up just as the long black sedan stopped, but I knew at once that it was Heshie coming for me. He stopped for a minute to say something to Mrs. Goldstein at the cash register. She turned to face me with a look of horror at what I was about to hear. Heshie hurried into the office, eased me out of my chair, and said, "You have to come home now."

He was steering me with his elbow at my arm, pushing me, for I was unable to move alone. The phone on my desk started to ring. Without thinking, I put out my hand, but he brushed it away and swept me toward the door, urging me almost into a run out to the street and into the car. He hurried around to slide in next to me.

"It's Samuel, Rebecca. He was crossing the street. Or just stepping off the curb to cross. A car hit him. The doctor said he was killed instantly. The driver must have been speeding to beat the light."

"Killed?" Heshie turned the key to start the engine. "Samuel? Dead? Only old people die. You must be wrong."

"There was no one else to tell you." His eyes were full of tears, but he blinked fast so he could keep on driving. "Your mother was home alone when a reporter for the *Daily Mirror* called. Then he caught me at my house. S-Samuel must have had a handbill for the theater in his pocket. You know how proud he . . . is—of our names on the notices. I answered the phone, and he wanted to know why Samuel was in the city. I hung up on him and ran over to your house. Your father was running up the hill when I got there."

"In all this heat," I said foolishly.

"I don't think he noticed. He can't leave your mother. So I said I would get the car and bring you home."

The car stopped in front of the house. Tears poured from the bruised marrow of my bones. Heshie sat patting my shoulder, crying next to me on the front seat of the black car. Finally he said, "I think we have to go up. Your mother and father need us. Try to stop enough to get up the stairs. In the house it will be all right again."

All right to cry, I thought. *Never all right to do anything else again.* Up the steps. Twenty, twenty-one, twenty-two, twenty-three, twenty-four. The only way I could climb was to count.

Papa and Mama, their faces rubbed to a blurred red similarity, held each other at the far end of the sofa. I fell down on the rug in front of them with my head where their knees met. We sobbed together, rocking back and forth.

I heard the phone ring and stop, the doorbell peal, and footsteps recede. All this happened not on the other side of a wall or door, but far away in another time and place.

(150)

I saw my brother marching up to the school, where Janet and I and two others waited, spinning on his heel and waving us on our way to protect the cemetery. Had he spun like that, one arm thrown aloft by the impact, when he was hit?

Ed Feldman came. Mama and Papa and I lifted our heads and let him talk to us about the arrangements. He would go to the funeral home, see about a plot, talk to the rabbi. We nodded, only eager for him to be gone so we could cry some more.

Later people came who spoke to us, tried to get us to eat, to drink, to talk. To each we said the least we could, drawing back before they had left the room. Only Heshie stayed, busy with the phone and the door, telling the story again. I could almost know the words he used from the rhythm of his speech, strained through the walls of our house and the sound of our tears.

Much later he urged us all up to our rooms, making sure each of us first swallowed a small blue pill. When I woke in the morning, my face was wet. I was pressed down against the mattress by the weight of a nameless sorrow. I did not want to move but lay there, letting it squeeze more tears from my endless supply. Gradually I remembered why I had been crying. Then I knew I had to get up to see if I could help Mama and Papa get ready.

Although I could hear the sounds of Mama's sobs beyond the wall, I could also hear the rattle of dishes in the kitchen. A stranger was there. When I got to the bottom of the steps, Tanta Greenbaum came out of the kitchen and opened her arms to me. Finally she asked, "Is Mama still asleep?" I shook my head. "All right, I'll go now to her. First you come with me to the kitchen. You must have something. A piece of roll, plain coffee. Then I'll bring Mama down. Meyer was up early. Uncle went with him to the *shul* already."

She led me to the table and put down a roll that she must have brought with her from the city, and a steaming cup of coffee in one of Mama's best *milchedig* cups. Instinct or memory must have guided her to the right dishes. As she set them before me, she talked. "We came in the night. I had to wait until Uncle could close the store. Your friend Hershel was asleep on the sofa when we got here. He made me take the sofa and he went to his own house. He said he didn't mind walking so late, he did it all the time. Uncle wanted to take him, but he said not to bother. Max is sorry he couldn't come with us. We had to leave him with the store. He wanted to be here. But I said it was more important for me to have his father here. He is more help to Meyer. And Max should watch things at home so we can stay as long as we're needed. You sit. I'm going to help Mama. In one hour they'll come to get us."

I had been able to look into Tanta's face. She had come to help. But what would happen when Mama came down? Could I look at her and still hold on to the little pieces that were fighting to break away? Would I dissolve into the horror? Was Mama upstairs worrying about the first sight of me and of Papa, who must have left while she still sorrowed in her drugged sleep?

I stood up when Tanta led Mama to the kitchen. We

met at its center and held each other up. "Meyer," Mama said through dry, peeling lips. "We must help Meyer."

"We will," I said, going back to my seat. Yes, I thought. That's how we do it. The functions take over. The comforting daughter replaces Rebecca so they can bear to look at me. The parents who need help lie like masks over the Sophie and Meyer who have known a grief that can never be assuaged so that I can bear to see their bereaved faces.

We sat across the table from each other, letting Tanta force bits of roll and sips of coffee into us. It would be a long day.

The funeral parlor was full of people who spoke to us, but they seemed like extras, hired to fill the hall in a drama in which, through some monumental error, I had been thrust on stage.

I was hot in my navy-blue dress with its high collar and long sleeves. For a moment I wondered if Samuel was hot in his navy-blue serge suit. Then I remembered. Until that moment I had been able to forget why I was there. "If I sit very still, my skin will hold me together," I thought. I sat still on the wooden folding seat, and the skin held through the rabbi's words. I sat still in the back of Ed Feldman's car as we drove down Easton Street and on along the river, and my skin held, although I could feel it stretched to bursting by the pressure. Then came the time to stand and to walk to the new grave.

It was at the end of the fourth row of stones, far from Abraham's. Remembering being there as a foot soldier in Samuel's army slowed my steps on the way to bury him. I felt someone take my arm. It was Tanta, who with barely audible words was walking me onward. A stronger touch, Heshie's, moved me along as he had at the store. "Just a little more," I thought I heard him say. "A little more . . . a little more . . . a little more" kept me from hearing what mustn't be heard and seeing what mustn't be seen.

Twenty-one, twenty-two, twenty-three, twenty-four, went the steps. Tanta hurried ahead. Before we could go into the house, the white porcelain basin with its pockmarked edge was brought out so we could wash our hands. Black ribbons were pinned on our clothes and then cut.

Inside the mirrors had been draped. In the living room three wooden crates waited to be seats for the mourners —Mama and Papa and me. We took off our shoes, and Tanta brought us our soft felt house slippers. The boxes were crowded in. Two were placed next to chairs, one near the faded maroon sofa. Someone urged me down to my box. Janet sat on the big mohair chair next to it. She could not help me, so I tried to make it easier for her. "At least we don't have a bed to move." She smiled sadly and quickly.

With relief she asked me if I had seen this one or that at the service, naming a long list of students. I could not tell her that my skin would have burst, spilling me all over the room, if I had let myself see and hear. Instead I admitted to seeing some and missing others so that she could think she was distracting me.

For a week, every day except the Sabbath, when we walked slowly to the *shul* and back, they came. Neighbors, former neighbors, friends, Mr. and Mrs. Goldstein,

Miss Robinson and Mr. Crawford from school, the cashier from the Strand, the Feldmans, Mrs. Morris, Mr. Whyte, the city engineer. Mama, Papa, and I looked and listened and talked without seeing, hearing or thinking. Uncle left but promised to come back for Tanta, who insisted she would stay with us for the week of mourning.

Then came the last *minyan*. Tanta, apologizing for the haste but adding that unless they left quickly, they would have to drive too long in the dark, kissed us and left. After them the others hurried back to their own lives. Could we look at each other now, I wondered? I tried, turning to face Mama and Papa. Yes, but not fully. Quick, glancing views, not direct—lest sorrow connect with sorrow and explode our careful constructions.

In the silence of the house Papa spoke first. "Now we have to go back to living. Sophie, Rebecca, we are still a family. We still all need each other. Each one must help the other." He spoke slowly, as though they were not his words but those of someone else, offered for his evaluation. Mama and I nodded. We needed to believe him.

After dinner the three of us sat in the living room as we had at the table, each in turn making one statement unanswered by the others. Next we would share a pause. One who had not just spoken would say one line. Pause. New sentence. Pause. New sentence. Then we heard feet, soft and blurred on the concrete, loud and sharp against the wooden floorboards of the porch.

Heshie came in. We gave him the welcoming nods of puppets created with a single expression, neither a smile nor a frown, but an all-purpose neutral face.

"Maybe I shouldn't have come . . ." he started.

"No, no," the puppets mouthed in unison.

"I know I'm welcome. That's not what I mean. But about Samuel's trip to the city—I thought you should know. He had an idea that independent owners—little guys—should form a cooperative. To fight block-booking. That way, maybe we could show what *we* want, not what gets rammed down our throats. Samuel went to New York to try to convince other exhibitors to go along—"

"Samuel never thought just because things were done a certain way, that was the way they always had to be," Papa said. "Thank you for coming to tell us."

"What difference? What difference?" Mama asked.

"Besides everything we always knew about Samuel, now we know," Papa told her, "that at the end he was trying to make things a little better. Like always."

"It doesn't help," Mama said.

"But Heshie thought it might, and he wanted us to know," I said. I hoped Heshie would not think Mama was angry with him when he had done so much for us. I turned to him. "And I'm glad you came so we can thank you for everything. We wouldn't have been able . . . without you and Tanta and Uncle . . . in the beginning—"

He gestured to cut me off, so I stopped. We sat quietly in the living room then, fitting this new information into our picture of Samuel. Soon all the pieces would be in. We would be able to lock the plates in place permanently, for there wouldn't be any more. Then we would only have to push the appropriate button to receive a completed print. True, each succeeding image would be less sharp, but for a long time the outline at least would be as clear as we could bear.

At the Smart Set Mr. and Mrs. Goldstein tried to be kind. "Do you need more time off?" Mr. Goldstein asked.

"Or maybe you should leave early so you don't tire yourself out at first?" his wife added.

"It's all right. I think the more I have to do, the better off I'll be. But thank you just the same."

On Tuesday I remembered Mrs. Morris and phoned her from the store. "I won't come tomorrow. It'll be too hard for my parents to be all alone at supper so soon. Maybe next week."

Neither Mama nor Papa mentioned that they were surprised to have me at home on a Wednesday night. But I missed hearing Mrs. Morris berate Mr. Roosevelt about not moving fast enough to help the unemployed, to see that the poor had adequate medical care, and to ensure that every man who worked got a fair wage. She always made everything seem so necessary and so logical that she quite convinced me that it was only a matter of time before everything would be better.

In the hot kitchen the three of us were still unable to look at each other for long. Our conversations were islands of words in the midst of the pain. After I helped Mama with the dishes, we moved out to the porch. The three of us shared the glider. I felt the tears struggling as I realized why we all fit.

Nobody had ever told me that this was what it was like when someone died—as though a great big hole were carved out of me. I felt an enormous emptiness of which I was reminded dozens of times a day. I would turn to see

Samuel, or to think of what he might say, or feel, or think, and he wouldn't be there.

Just a boy, a child, who never had a chance to do anything. Who had heard a voice that called him to sample the riches of the world but had scarcely had a chance to respond. Now it was over. He had been stopped in his work before he could even discover what it was. We would have to learn to live with the empty space in all of our lives, to try to make some sense of what happened.

I wished then that I believed in Heaven, that I could think that someday we would be reunited, Mama and Papa and Samuel and I. Yes, even baby Abraham. I thought of the plain pine box that Samuel had been in and where the box was now. The tears streamed down, until I saw that Mama was crying too. I knew I must stop. There had to be an end.

On the sidewalk Janet appeared in the circle of light from the streetlamp. I ran in to wash my face and catch my breath so that I would be able to talk to her.

"I thought we should walk down by the river. It's cooler there," she said after a few words with my parents.

"That river is only cool in the winter," I told her. "In the summer I can get hot just looking at it steam."

Janet was not to be put off. "Okay then. Up the hill past the Wallingtons'. It's always cool near the woods."

"Go, Rebecca," Mama said. "You sit all day at a desk. You need a little exercise."

"It's a good thing there isn't a turnstile we have to drop some money in before we can take a walk. Then there wouldn't be anything at all we could afford to do."

"Walking is just an excuse to get you off the porch,"

my friend said reasonably, not letting my anger offend
her. "You have to get back to normal a little bit at a
time." Normal, I wanted to shout to her. What's normal
about boys dying? Not old men like your father, but
young boys.

"Why?"

"Because you can't stay at home and shut out the
world."

"The world comes and gets you no matter where you
are." I thought of sitting behind the half glass, watching
the Greenspans' black sedan coming for me. Any black
car that passed me now brought back the terrible drop
of everything inside me that had happened when Heshie
rushed past Mrs. Goldstein.

A small breeze rose from the trees behind the Wallingtons' house as we followed the footpath up the hill. The
leaves whispered to each other that strangers were coming into their woods. We walked.

"How can Mama and Papa stand it?" I asked Janet.
"Twice to lose a son."

"I think it's because they know they still have to look
after you."

Finally I told Janet that I thought I should get back to
my parents. She answered that the next night we would
walk some more. I was peeved that Janet had not understood that I wanted to be left to myself. She seemed to
have forgotten her pain at being shut out of my plans to
go to college.

She said good-bye at the bottom of our steps. I climbed
them, thinking of school for the first time since I had
seen Heshie coming for me at the Smart Set. I knew then

that it would be impossible for me to leave in six weeks. Abandoning Papa to solitary climbs up from Easton Street for dinner. Sentencing Mama and Papa to hours of just the two of them across from each other at the table that had so recently held four. The sweet scent of browned onions hovering over untouched food. The room whispering with unspoken words. Sorrow wilting the freshly ironed tablecloths in the buffet drawers, clouding the shiny jars of homemade jam and home-canned peaches that lined the pantry shelves.

Next year when we had at last learned to look at each other, to have devised a protective coloration before the rest of the world, then I could think of going off every day. Now, however, I could not leave the parents who needed me.

Chapter 12

The next morning I told Mr. Goldstein of my decision. "Whatever you want is all right with me. Part-time I can use you. Full-time, if that's what you want, I can use you too."

When Janet came for me after dinner, I told her I wanted to visit Mrs. Morris briefly. Janet agreed that we could go together and she would wait to walk me home. I left her sitting just across from the house on a white-washed boulder that had formerly marked the entrance to the estate.

The bell rang in the dark hall. Mrs. Morris was a long time in answering. Finally I heard footsteps brushing hesitantly on the polished floor.

The smile she gave me was swift and sure. "Ah, Rebecca, how nice. It was quiet here Wednesday. I hope you are going to tell me you can come next week. Help me carry out some chairs so we can sit out here. It's too hot inside."

"Just one for you. I'd rather sit here." I pointed to the top step.

I leaned back against the column supporting the porch roof. Facing me, Mrs. Morris sat on a finely turned walnut chair that, like its owner, looked like a delicate line drawing of itself. "How are your parents?" she asked.

I nodded. Words said too little and too much. I thought I'd better tell her quickly. "I've asked Mr. Goldstein if I can work full-time over the winter. I can't go away to school now. Maybe next year."

She understood before I had finished speaking. "Just Mr. Goldstein? You haven't told the school?"

I nodded again.

"Please, promise me one thing. I never asked a favor of you before. Don't tell them yet. It's only the end of July. The middle of August will still be a full month before classes start."

"I'm afraid to wait. I might change my mind."

"That's what I'm hoping for. Please do it. Just wait two weeks. After that I'll even help you write the letter turning them down. If that will make it easier to do."

"If I say I'll wait, that means I'm not sure. But I am sure. It's the right thing to do."

"Sometimes it's better not to do the right thing. Remember, I never asked you for a favor before. I think you owe me that."

"All right. I'll wait. But only as a favor to you."

Turning the Corner

As I walked to meet Janet I remembered Mrs. Morris telling me months ago that it was important never to lie to myself. I wondered if it was possible ever to be sure why I did anything. I knew, however, that I must believe that waiting these two weeks was a favor to Mrs. Morris, granted only as an obligation of friendship.

Johnny Waite's cab hardly ever came to our house. So Mama and Papa and I watched carefully from the porch to see who would alight. It was Mrs. Morris, her hair crested by the breeze, the seams of her Bemberg sheer dress awry on her bony shoulders, her belt twisted at the side. I heard her tell Johnny to come back in an hour and a half as I hurried to help her up the steps.

At the top she paused to catch her breath. "Let's stay here," she said, turning back Mama's suggestion that we would be more comfortable in the living room.

First I pulled out the chair from the hall. Then I left again for one from the dining room. When three of us were on the glider, as we had been before, there was really no way to talk, for each faced straight ahead. We had preferred sitting that way. But Mrs. Morris had come to make me change my mind, and four people would be confronting each other from separate corners. I dawdled with the second chair, trying to plan a strategy to resist her.

Mama, Papa, and Mrs. Morris had finished with the weather as I slowly brought the chair out. Mrs. Morris now announced the purpose of her visit. "Has Rebecca told you that she's decided not to go to college in September?"

(163)

Papa and Mama turned toward me as I squirmed in the chair I had just set down. I tried to think of ways to explain why I had not told them myself. They shook their heads.

"I'm sorry to upset you. But I need your help to make her change her mind."

"If she thinks she shouldn't go, then maybe it's not such a bad idea she shouldn't," Mama said. "I always worried she was trying to do too much."

Papa turned to Mrs. Morris. "Tell us, please, why you think it's important Rebecca should learn to be a teacher?"

"If Rebecca stays here, what future does she have? Being the best bookkeeper in Forgetown?"

"She won't work forever. She'll meet a nice boy and get married. And why not?" asked Mama.

"And until she does, her brain will atrophy."

"Wait, wait, ladies. Let's let Rebecca tell her side."

"Well . . . this isn't such a good time to go. I can wait and save up a little money and go next year."

Papa summed up. "But Mrs. Morris is worried that if you wait a year, then you'll never go."

"I don't think so, Pa. It'll just be easier next year."

"What's the rush? If next year is better," Mama said, "let it be next year."

"Next year, next year," Papa answered. "I think Mrs. Morris is right. Next year could be never."

"Thank you, Meyer. I'm glad you understand."

Papa resumed. "Of course, if Rebecca is sure what she wants, then a year won't matter much."

"But she's already a year behind."

"I know, I know. So let's say, Rebecca, you'll think it over. Also Mama and I will think about it. And for a week or two, we'll let it be like that."

We all knew Papa was saying we needed time to be able to face my being away from home most days and evenings. But I could not forget the winter nights that would come in icy blasts across the river, when the three of us would wish I were safely in the house rather than fighting my way there from the station or the Smart Set. And other nights when Papa and I would be off on our separate ways, while the quiet would leer at Mama from the corners of the rooms. Or worse, Mama and Papa would sit home together with no one to ease them over the gaps in their conversation.

"Pa, I think I decided right the first time."

"It could be. But what's wrong with waiting two weeks to make sure about such an important thing?"

"Two weeks sounds right," said Mrs. Morris. "We'll all be thinking clearer then."

Mama looked at her as though to indicate she was satisfied with the way people were thinking now, but said nothing. Papa suggested we could all use a cold drink. While Mama was getting the iced tea, Papa and Mrs. Morris started to talk about 1940, the next presidential year. Mr. Thomas would run again, they thought. So would President Roosevelt. I thought about 1940 too. Papa would be nearly sixty; Mrs. Morris, eighty-five. How could they be here and alive and planning for the future when my little brother had no future anymore?

Mrs. Morris looked up as I passed her a cold, beaded glass. "Maybe you should think about going into government, Rebecca. They could use some clear-thinking people in Washington." Nothing stopped her plans for me.

"It'll be a long time before I'll be trained for anything."

"It may seem long now. But the future always surprises us by how soon it comes."

When Johnny Waite drove up, I ran to tell him Mrs. Morris would be there in a minute. Papa helped her from her chair and slowly down the twenty-four steps.

As the car drove away Heshie walked through the pool of light from the streetlamp. He had probably been waiting, in the dark farther down the hill, for Mrs. Morris to leave. I wondered if he had tried to guess what we had been discussing.

"It's not late yet, Rebecca. Would you like to come for a ride and cool off?"

I shook my head. I would not be able to enter that car for a long time. "I'll walk a little, if you're not too tired. I've been sitting all evening."

Walking was easier than facing each other across a room, for it was necessary to watch where we placed our feet as we alternately entered patches of light and dark. I would not be able to look at Heshie's open Greenspan face for a long time either.

"I know you must wish it had been me," he said.

"I never thought that," I said truthfully. I had not considered that I might have bartered for my brother's life with his friend's. "But thank you for telling me. So I can tell you it isn't so. It just never occurred to me. That kind of thinking doesn't make sense."

"Just because it doesn't make sense doesn't keep peo-

ple from doing it all the time. They'll trade off anything
to save themselves and the ones closest to them."

"Maybe so. But I didn't think of it and I don't want to
talk about it."

"What can we talk about?" He had not reached out
to touch me. Neither of us was ready for that.

"The weather? Baseball? But you'll have to explain
about the leagues and all so I know what's going on."
The list of subjects we could not discuss was much longer
than those we could. Then I decided that Heshie should
know that I had changed my mind. "Maybe you guessed.
I'm not going to go to school next year."

"Is that what she was over your house about? That
Mrs. Morris?"

"She says I should go on as I planned to before."

"I'll bet she does. What do your folks say?"

"That I should wait two weeks to decide."

"If you don't go and aren't busy all the time, then
maybe you could come to the theater after work some
nights."

"Well, I won't be busy with homework."

"I'm glad you don't wish it was me." We had turned
and were about to start back. Heshie put his arms out
and pulled me to him. My body surprised and angered
me by being ready to be excited by his kiss. I did not let
him do it again.

That night I dreamed of a giant ballroom. I was a
partner, passed hand to hand—to Mama, Papa, Mrs.
Morris, Heshie, to someone without a face who I knew
was Samuel. No sooner would my partner and I start
spinning gracefully in one direction than a new partner

would whirl me off in another. The music urged us to greater speed and more intricate steps, but no one smiled or seemed to be having a good time. When I awoke, I was hot and tired. I took a cold bath to wash away the night's exertion so that I could get dressed for work.

Two nights before the two weeks were up Papa, pushing away his half-eaten dinner, said he and Mama had decided I should go to school as I had originally planned.

"Are you sure you talked to Mama about it? Or is this your idea?"

"All right, so it's mostly my idea, but I'm sure Mama feels the same." Mama nodded grudgingly, I thought.

"Aren't I old enough to know what I want?" I asked.

"No. Eighteen, even nineteen, is too young to know. But people go ahead and make plans that could change a whole life."

"I've only decided to wait a year."

"You think it will be easier for Mama and me if you go next year instead. But it won't. It will be just as hard. It's easier to know that you'll be doing what you started to do before. . . ."

This, then, was what I had contracted for when I had agreed to wait. Papa and Mrs. Morris had danced me to the gates of the outside world. I would begin to fill up the empty places inside me with new faces and new ideas. Mama and Papa would stay behind with memories of what they had lost.

The nineteenth of September was so bright and blue that it hurt my eyes as I stepped off the porch on my way to catch the seven thirty train.

Mama and Papa had gotten up to have breakfast with me. They watched me from the porch. I waved as I turned the corner out of their sight. My gray skirt had twisted as I moved, and I straightened it. The skirt and blouse were old. But for the first time in my life all my underwear was brand-new, crisp and silky against my skin.

On the platform there were a dozen men in business suits who looked as though they made the trip every day. There were women in dark dresses who seemed to be performing important errands. And there was Rebecca Levine starting on a new life in her old gray skirt.

I entered the last car just as the conductor finished flipping the seatbacks into a face-front position. I slid across the slippery rattan to get close to the window. The polished seat that felt cool and refreshing would probably be cold and uninviting in the winter. The other passengers, the sounds, the smells, would soon be as familiar as home.

We began to pick up speed. I clutched my new notebook, black leather with a zipper all around—a gift from Mrs. Morris—and the brown pocketbook I had just finished paying Mrs. Goldstein for. The tracks followed the river for nearly a mile. When I looked back, all I could see was the Works' buildings clustering at the water's edge.

I turned around to face front. I knew then that the goings and comings would not cancel each other out. That, although I would return as often as I left, the net result would be more leaving than returning, as though the going was more important, so that at the end of my four years at school, I would already be away. The Works, the cemetery with both my brothers, the Smart Set, the intersection of Broadway and Easton Street, the Wallingtons' house on the crest, our house resting on twenty-four steps from whose risers the traces of RED and JEW had finally disappeared, Janet at the five-and-ten, Mrs. Morris in her living room, Mama and Papa watching from the porch, were already growing dim only five miles down the road of the very first trip.